Ris

CLAIRE KENT

ONE

Only fuck a man if he can do something for you.

That had been the first piece of advice Talia had received last year after entering the leisure suite, and she reminded herself to follow it nearly every day.

The hardest thing was figuring out which men could actually do her some good.

The leisure suite was only available to high-ranking Coalition officials or guests of the Residence of the High Director. All the men and women who had access were either rich or powerful—most of them were both. But sometimes the richest and most powerful people were also the stingiest with their money. They would refuse to offer donations to the suite in exchange for using its services.

Fucking a man who wouldn't donate afterward was a wasted effort. Talia had made a number of those mistakes when she'd first arrived, and she was trying not to do it again.

She needed to fuck men who would do her some good—who would donate generously to the suite afterward—and it took practice and discernment to recognize which ones would.

She'd only been here for eleven months. She still had a lot of learning left to do.

"Try not to look so eager," Jenelle murmured to her softly, leaning over so no one else in their section could hear her words. "Men are contrary, and most won't want a girl who is easy to get."

Talia groaned and leaned back in her seat. She and Jenelle were sitting in the leisure suite section of the central arena, where the next round of the Combat Tournament was about to begin. Talia didn't really care for watching the fighting, but she needed to attend each of the weekly rounds anyway. The arena was packed. Everyone who had any status in the Coalition and was currently stationed on Earth or its surroundings was here. If she wanted to attract another man this week, this was where she would find him tonight. "Why did they even choose me for the suite? I'm terrible at this."

Jenelle laughed. She was in her early thirties and was both beautiful and intelligent. She'd been assigned as Talia's mentor when she'd first started in the suite last year, and she was still her friend. "You're not terrible. Everyone has been very pleased with your services, and most of them have offered donations afterward."

"Not very big ones though." The suite might be designed to offer sexual favors to the Coalition Council and the High Director's guests, but it was no different from any other workplace. In order to move up in the suite hierarchy and earn a better room, nicer clothes, and more replicator privileges, leisure escorts had to earn donations.

The larger the donations, the more privileges they earned.

Right now Talia was sharing a room with eight other girls—a step up from the common room she'd had to sleep in when she first arrived.

Eventually she wanted her own room like Jenelle. Real privacy in a space larger than the sleeping pod she currently possessed. Absolute quiet. Maybe even an allowance to purchase a few treats now and then. Real fruit. Even chocolate.

She'd never had her own room in her life, and right now the only food she could eat was the replicated stuff—food processed from base nutrients and designed to look and taste like the real thing. It was a far better replicator quality than what she'd had to eat as a child, but still... It simply couldn't come close to real food.

But the only way to get her own room and an allowance was to earn as many donations as Jenelle earned, which meant she had to become the favorite of a powerful man.

Jenelle only fucked one man now. He was a trusted advisor to the High Director, and he donated enough to the suite to make it worth Jenelle's seeing him exclusively. He was in his sixties and not particularly attractive, but he was kind, and Jenelle actually liked him.

It sounded like a dream to Talia. Only one man to fuck—and a nice one. Her own room. A little bit of freedom. Her goal was to get there before she was thirty, which meant she had twelve years left to go.

She'd never get there, though, if only the losers were interested in her.

"Stop worrying," Jenelle told her, evidently reading her mind. "You're doing just fine."

"Sure I am. I've only fucked three men all week. Most of them aren't interested in me. My body just isn't right."

Jenelle shook her head. "Stop it with that. You know very well that we need a variety of body types because different men and women all have unique tastes. Some men prefer bodies like yours."

Talia believed that in theory. On her home planet, men had started staring at her with hunger in their eyes when she was fourteen years old. She had large breasts and rounded hips and a heart-shaped face. She'd grown up understanding her value was in her physical beauty, whether or not she always liked what she saw in the mirror.

It was different on Earth though. Everyone was sophisticated and cynical here, and they all followed whatever body type happened to be in fashion.

What was in fashion right now for women were elegant, slim bodies and slight curves in keeping with the life partner of the High Director. The slimmer, the better. Jenelle was built like that, as were a good number of the female escorts in the leisure suite.

Talia wasn't fat or even overweight. She didn't earn enough donations to eat much real food, and you couldn't get fat on replicated food. But she was too curvy to be of interest to most men. Even the men who might have been attracted to her still didn't choose her because they were trying to follow the current trends.

People were like clones, and the closer one got to the center of Coalition power, the more like clones people became.

The Residence of the High Director of the Coalition Council was as close to the center of power as one could get in the explored universe.

Older men—most of them over seventy—seemed to like her the most, and she was perfectly fine with that. Even with artificial aids, men that age rarely expected very vigorous sex. Some of them just liked to have a warm body in bed with them.

She was happy to be a warm body. It didn't take any practiced skills for that, so her inexperience wasn't a problem.

All she needed to do was find a generous old man who wanted to see her regularly, and she would be set.

When a gray-haired man walked by the leisure suite section, eyeing the women (there were also plenty of men in the leisure suite, but this man obviously preferred women), Talia straightened up.

"Not too eager," Jenelle murmured.

Talia did her best to compose her expression into one of cool disinterest, as if whether this man chose her wasn't a significant matter. When he paused in front of her, she moved her hand to the tie of her tunic so she could open it and show him her breasts to let him know she was available, but he moved on before she could.

She slumped back, watching as he ended up making an appointment with Breann, who was a few years older than her and had a similar body type to her.

Breann had the reputation of being very skillful in bed.

Talia hadn't been here long enough to develop those kinds of skills.

"Don't worry about it," Jenelle said with an encouraging smile. "He looks like he's tight-fisted anyway, so he'd probably be a waste of time."

Talia was happy to hear that. She never doubted it was true because Jenelle was much better at reading men than she was.

"The fights are about to start," Jenelle added, turning Talia's attention to the masked Combatants who were filing out into the ten combat rings on the floor of the arena.

The ten fights in tonight's round would occur at the same time. These Combatants had been whittled down from the hundred who began the Tournament three weeks ago. After tonight, the winners would go on to fight next week and so on until there was just one fight in the final round and then just one Combatant remaining.

The Tournament only took place every four years, so this was the first one Talia had been present for.

The fights were no-holds-barred, and they usually ended up bloody. Talia really didn't like to watch the raw, violent grappling. Sometimes it nauseated her. She hoped it wouldn't be too bad tonight, and she kept her eyes on the two men fighting in the ring closest to where she sat.

She was surprised when, in less than a minute, one of the men was down and not moving.

Tournament fights almost never ended so quickly.

The crowd was cheering for the winning Combatant, and he raised a hand in victory. He got to go on to next week's round, and he hadn't even been injured. He was barely sweating.

He wasn't as big as most of the other Combatants, although his muscle development was very impressive. He had hair on his chest, which was unusual since most of the Combatants shaved themselves clean.

"This must be his first Tournament," Jenelle said, eyeing the man. "He looks young, and I'm sure he wasn't here four years ago. I wonder where he came from."

Talia was mildly impressed with the man's easy victory, but she wasn't interested enough to pay him much attention. Her eyes were roaming the aisles near where she sat again, hoping for a man to appear who was interested in her.

Three fucks in one week weren't nearly enough to earn her an improvement in lifestyle. She didn't like the girls she shared the room with, but she also didn't like being trapped in her sleeping pod, which was the only way she could be alone in her current circumstances.

If she could earn more donations, she could at least move up to a room with just three other girls and a bigger pod.

Two years ago, back in her home village, she'd never believed even that much was possible in her life.

Things were different now. She could expect more than the loneliness and barren drudgery she'd grown up with.

But it would never happen if no one looked at her twice.

~

Talia didn't get another man that evening, and she didn't have any appointments the following day. She had to sit in the common room and hope for a drop-in to choose her, but by midafternoon, she was so tired of listening to the endless chattering of the other escorts that she went to hide in the library for a few hours.

The Residence of the High Director might sound like it was a house, but it wasn't. It was a fortress as large as a city that orbited Earth. It boasted the best that Coalition civilization had to offer. As an escort, Talia didn't have access to most of the perks, but she was allowed to use the library.

The Residence library had digital access to the entire public Coalition archive. But it also had more than that.

It had real books. Actual bound books with paper pages. Talia was allowed to read them. And she was even allowed to borrow them and take them with her as long as she scanned them out so there was a record of who had them.

As far as she was concerned, the best part of becoming a leisure escort was having access to the library.

Talia loved books, and she loved reading, but she often went to be alone. To have quiet for a little while, away from everyone else.

She'd never seen anyone else in the library in the eleven months she'd been living at the Residence.

When she'd been a girl in her home village, her favorite thing had been to visit a nice old man who had a shelf of historical books. The books were all about past civilizations that had thrown off oppressive regimes and found freedom.

The old man had let her read his books, and she'd read them over and over again. She loved those stories. She knew most of them by heart. She'd spent hours daydreaming about stories like that coming true in her own world, although she knew it was impossible. So she always searched the Residence library for more stories like that.

She didn't care if they were real history or not. She liked to read of rebellions, of revolutions, of victory over oppression.

She liked to daydream it was possible.

Occasionally she read stories about the formation of the Coalition. A thousand years ago when space travel became safe, humans had spread from Earth to ever-expanding regions of space, populating planets and developing new worlds. They'd brought their cultural differences and ideological divisions with them, however, and eventually they'd established the Coalition Council as a way of maintaining peace.

The Council included a representative from all the major planets, and it was supposed to support justice and freedom for all the worlds under its governance. Hundreds of years had passed since then however, and none of the old ideals still held.

The Coalition Council was filled with the most ruthless and ambitious people, and the High Director was the worst of them all. Their only priority was to maintain power, and they did anything necessary to hold on to it. They didn't take care of people or worlds or anything really. They only kept control.

She'd always thought it was sad. Heartbreaking, really. That a government that had begun with good ideals had transformed into what it was now.

It was too depressing to read about it very much, so she usually went much farther back into early Earth cultures.

Earlier this week, she'd found a collection of ancient stories, many of which were about the enslaved becoming free. She grabbed the big volume off the shelf again and took it over to her favorite curtained window seat to read it.

She spent a happy hour reading about a beautiful woman who had become the concubine of an ancient king. She'd then become his queen. She'd then managed to save her people.

Talia loved the story so much she read it twice.

Eventually she forced herself to close the book.

She'd spent too long here already, and she needed to get back to the suite. She would never get anywhere unless she found a few partners, and she couldn't do that from the library. She grabbed a few books to read over the next evenings, in case she still didn't have any appointments, and then she left the library, mentally reviewing her list of men who'd shown interest in her and might want to see her again.

She always kept a running tally of those men in her mind, rehashing their age, appearance, wealth, and status, taking comfort in having as many possibilities as possible.

One day she was going to be a favorite.

One day she'd have her own room.

The hall was mostly empty in the midafternoon like this since the Council was in session. So she was surprised when she turned a corner and saw a man approaching her. He had dark blond hair and a square face and looked to be in his midthirties. Talia recognized him immediately.

Usually a man so young was of no interest to her since it took a long time to gain political power in the Coalition. But Talia recognized this one. He was one of the subcommanders of Coalition Special Forces, and he'd just arrived at the Residence a few days ago after being stationed on a border planet.

She gave him a little smile as she passed him.

She'd seen him at the Tournament last night, which was where she'd found out who he was. He hadn't shown her any interest, but that didn't mean he never would.

She wasn't naturally outgoing, but being shy didn't work for an escort. So she forced herself to say, "Good afternoon. Be sure to stop by the leisure suite when you have some free time."

He paused, causing her heart to jump in excitement.

His eyes crawled over her body from her high, dark ponytail to the toes of her boots—made in a soft fabric that molded her legs all the way to her midthighs. Most of the women in the leisure suite wore boots like that, and both men and women wore ponytails high on their heads. It was the way they were identified.

He didn't say anything, but he kept looking at her, so her hope intensified. She adjusted her stack of books to reveal more of her body and gave him a slightly trembling smile that she'd practiced for months with Jenelle. (Jenelle had always advised that Talia, with her long hair, youthful appearance, and dimples to put on a shy, girlish demeanor since a lot of men really liked that.) "We'd love to see you in the leisure suite," she said, dropping her eyelashes strategically.

When she looked back up, she was pleased to see that the man's expression had grown hot with interest. He reached out to raise her chin. "You're a little chubby for my taste, but it looks like you've got great tits."

Chubby.

Talia hated being called chubby.

Despite his words, this man didn't seem to mind her body. In fact, he'd moved his hand down to the neckline of her tunic, pulling it away from her skin so he could see what was beneath. He kept pulling until the fabric started to tear.

To make it easier for him and to keep him from ripping her tunic any more, she moved her books to one arm and untied her sash. The tunic was a wraparound, and she pulled it open to show him her breasts.

Her breasts were good. Everyone said so. They were big and rounded with perky rosy nipples. Her belly was soft but mostly flat, and her pussy was shaved smooth.

Her heart was racing in excitement as she waited for the man to make up his mind.

He was interested.

He was definitely interested.

And he wasn't gross or unattractive.

He was a subcommander in the Special Forces.

She couldn't have asked for anything better.

"Do you have a few minutes right now?" he asked at last, his voice slightly thick with lust.

She gave herself a mental cheer as she gave the man a slow smile. "For you? Of course I do."

He glanced around the hall, as if orienting himself to his location.

"We could go to one of the playrooms in the suite. Or the library is empty," she suggested, nodding toward a closed door.

That was another piece of advice she'd gotten from Talia. No matter where you were, always be conscious of places for men to fuck you since you never knew when the opportunity would arise.

The man put his hand on the back of her neck and guided her toward the door. He applied more pressure than necessary. She didn't need to be pushed.

This was the best thing to happen to her all year.

She wasn't going anywhere but that room.

When he closed the door behind them, he asked, "How are you with your mouth?"

"I'll let you be the judge of that," she said, flashing her dimple and lowering her lashes in another shy look after she'd put her stack of books on the table.

"Good." He pushed her down onto her knees, not gently but not roughly enough to bother her. The girls in the suite all knew the men who were inclined to hurt them and made sure to avoid them. Officially, a girl in the suite could say no whenever she wanted. It was on the books as an inviolable law—rape was illegal in any situation, including for the men and women who worked in the leisure suite.

In Coalition space, however, laws were often on the books simply for appearance's sake. And practically speaking, if she went around saying no to men who wanted to fuck her, she might as well call it quits and go back home.

Occasionally, if she'd had a bad day, she was tempted. She was allowed to leave if she wanted, as long as she went through a long exit process. Her family wouldn't have to pay back all the money they'd received when she'd been chosen for the leisure suite last year. It had been enough to provide for her family for the rest of their lives, and it wasn't contingent on her staying in the suite for any particular length of time.

But she had nothing to go home for—just a stark, joyless planet and a village of people who'd never really understood her. The old man with the books had died three years ago. He was the only real friend she'd had.

Plus her home planet was old-fashioned, and they'd likely all see her as a whore. She would hate that.

She had a better chance of a good life here, if she could get better at pleasing men.

The leisure suite was for life. When a woman got too old for men to want to fuck, then she stayed to help train the younger girls.

It was a better life than anything that would be waiting for her on her home planet, and the first step toward achieving it was pleasing this man in front of her.

She was so excited her heart was racing in her throat.

"I don't have much time," the man said matter-of-factly. "Take off your top first. I really like those big tits. And don't use your teeth."

Her tunic was still hanging open, so she let it slide off her arms. Then she unfastened his trousers and freed his cock, which was already mostly erect from looking at her breasts.

She wished he wasn't in a hurry so she could really give him a good time, but he'd said specifically that he only had a few minutes, so she wasn't going to be stupid and drag this out longer than he wanted.

She stroked his cock lightly and then teased it with her tongue, paying attention to what caused his thigh muscles to tighten and his breath to hitch.

Then she took him in her mouth fully. After the first few sucks, he hardened all the way.

He obviously wasn't a talker, which was fine with her. He made wordless sounds that proved he was enjoying this, and soon he started to rock his hips with the rhythm of her sucking.

She loosened her throat muscles as much as she could so she didn't choke when he pushed in deeper. He grabbed her ponytail with both hands and was holding on to it as she sucked him off.

She wasn't as practiced at this as a lot of women in the leisure suite. She'd only been here a year, and she'd been a virgin when she'd arrived—which had increased her value for obvious reasons. But she used every trick in her small arsenal to add to his pleasure. She massaged his balls and then the sensitive spot behind them, and that made him gasp and jerk.

"Fuck, you're good," he grunted. "Now I want to know if your pussy is as sweet as your mouth."

She couldn't respond with words since his cock was filling her mouth, but she raised her eyes to his face to see if this meant he wanted her to stop sucking him off.

He pulled her head back, letting his erection slip out of her mouth, and then he hauled her to her feet and turned her around, bending her over the table and pushing her shoulders down until her cheek was pressed again the cool metal.

She was naked except for her boots, and the edge of the table dug into her stomach uncomfortably, but she'd far rather have a man fuck her from behind than have him all in her face, so she was pleased with the position.

"Do you like it like this?" the man asked, parting her ass cheeks until he could find her pussy.

She normally met with men in the playrooms of the leisure suite, where there was always lubricant available. Jenelle had trained her to use sexual fantasies to arouse herself, but Talia had to focus so much on using all her skills that it was hard for her to fantasize at the same time. When she had time to prepare, she did it beforehand—imagining herself alone with a vibrator, which was the only way she'd ever come. She hadn't been able to do that this time, but she'd learned to relax her body completely. When the man wedged his cock into her pussy, she was surprised to find that she was a little wet.

She was so excited by the opportunity that her body must have reacted.

"Damn, your pussy is so hot and tight. How does that feel?" the man asked, rolling his hips. Maybe he was a talker after all. "You like the feel of me inside you, don't you?"

She'd learned very early that questions like this meant the man wanted affirmation and an ego boost.

Some women enjoyed sex, but she never had. She didn't hate it. She just didn't get pleasure out of it. She'd certainly never had an orgasm with a man.

She wasn't stupid enough to let men see this though.

So she made her voice breathless and said, "Yeah. Oh yeah, it feels so good!" When he pushed into her with a hard thrust, she gave a little cry, like it had felt so good she couldn't hold back.

She stretched her arms spread-eagle on the table, palms flat, as he thrust again. Then she started up a series of vocal responses as he fucked her hard. She babbled in a broken, girlish voice about how good he was, how big he was, how much he was going to make her come. She could fake it pretty well now, so she tightened her pussy around his penetration and gradually increased the decibel of her cries.

He wanted affirmation, so that meant he'd probably want her to come.

He was holding on to her ponytail with one hand and gripping one side of her bottom with the other. With each thrust, his pelvis slapped against the soft flesh of her ass, making a rhythmic spanking sound.

He was getting louder. And faster. And rougher.

His grip on her hair was starting to hurt.

But he was liking this. A lot. She looked at him over her shoulder to make sure, and there was no mistaking his flushed face, his contorted features, the tension in his shoulders and arms.

He was liking this a lot.

She made a loud sobbing sound and shook her body in tight shudders, as if she'd reached climax.

"Yeah," the man grunted, "Oh yeah. I can feel that hot pussy coming for me. You're taking it so good."

He leaned over, letting go of her bottom and bracing himself on the table. The move changed the penetration.

Her stomach was really hurting from the edge of the table now, and her breasts were smashed on the cold, hard surface, her nipples rubbing against it as he moved her body with his thrusts. He was pulling on her hair still, but she could tell he was nearing the end.

Since he seemed to like to hear how much she was enjoying it, she kept up her gasps and babbles. "So good, so good, you're giving it to me so good. Gonna come again."

He really liked that last one. He almost roared and gave her a sharp slap on one side of her bottom.

She squeezed her pussy around him as hard as she could and screamed with what she hoped sounded like pleasure.

Finally he let go, giving another roar and falling out of rhythm.

He released himself into her. It felt like there was a lot of semen.

She wondered how long it had been since he'd had sex.

He'd been on the border until this week. He'd only arrived at the Residence a few days ago.

And he'd fucked *her*.

He'd chosen *her*.

He'd really seemed to like it.

She gasped and wheezed as he pulled out of her and gave her bottom an approving pat. "Maybe I like the chubby ones after all. All that jiggling is pretty hot."

That was a compliment. Not a nice one but still a compliment. So she was smiling as she straightened up, hiding her cringe as her muscles stretched painfully at the move.

She was going to have a bruise across her belly, but it would be worth it if he wanted to fuck her again.

"I'm glad you enjoyed it," she told him breathlessly. She knew her cheeks were red, and she let her long, dark ponytail swing forward as if she were trying to hide her face.

He pushed her hair back with a smug smile. "Don't try to hide it from me. I saw how hard you came. You've obviously needed a real man to give it to you good for a long time. Nothing to be embarrassed about."

She fluttered her lashes, pretending a shyness she didn't feel. "I've never come so hard before. And twice," she whispered.

He chuckled and gave her bottom one more little spank, harder than before. "I'm going to look for you again. And we'll see how many more times you can come when I have more time."

She smiled but kept her lashes lowered.

Hopefully he would give the leisure suite a donation to show his appreciation.

If men used the suite but didn't give donations, then the men and women who worked there would stop offering those men their services. Everyone knew that, so most people would donate at least a little.

This man was a subcommander. Maybe he would donate a lot.

If he wanted to think he could make her feel like no one else ever would, then that was what she would let him think.

He was a man, and men could be easily manipulated.

This one was no exception.

She wished she could remember his name.

She couldn't wait to tell Jenelle how well she'd done this afternoon.

And he'd said he was going to look for her again.

She let him leave first. Then she closed her tunic and tied the sash, shaking her head over the ripped fabric. It could be fixed. It was good that he was enthusiastic about seeing her body. She was sore and stiff and flushed and uncomfortable. She needed to clean herself up between the legs, and her tunic was torn.

But none of that mattered.

If the subcommander liked her, then maybe he would want to keep seeing her.

Maybe she could become his favorite.

She was only eighteen, and she was still new to this, but she thought she'd done pretty well.

When she'd pulled herself back together, Talia collected her stack of books and once more left the library to head to the leisure suite.

Jenelle was probably having a drink in the garden right now. Talia started to hurry so she could tell her friend her good news.

She hadn't yet reached the suite when a transport roared up behind her, far too fast for an interior corridor, and barely swerved to miss her.

The suddenness of it startled her, and Talia jumped away from the transport awkwardly as it zoomed by.

She fell against a closed door and dropped her books.

She cursed the selfish idiot who was in such a hurry.

She was kneeling on the floor, collecting her fallen books, when the door she'd bumped into slid open.

Looking up, she saw a tall man looming above her. He wore the soft, thin trousers and tunic that were common daytime wear around the Residence. He was barefoot, and as she looked up his body, she blinked when she saw he wore a Combatant's mask.

"Are you all right?" he asked, looking down at her. His hair was light brown, and his body was very strong. She couldn't tell anything more about his appearance because of his mask.

"Yes. I'm fine. Thank you." She felt like an idiot as she hastily restacked her books. Leave it to her to make a fool of herself in front of a Combatant.

When she glanced up at him, she suddenly realized that he was the one who had won so quickly last night. He wasn't hugely bulky like most of the others, and the slight cleft in his chin was distinct.

She was reaching for her last book, focused on getting back on her feet, when she discovered he'd leaned over to pick it up for her.

She discovered this when she nearly knocked heads with him.

Feeling even more like an idiot, she jerked backward to avoid the collision.

She fell clumsily on her ass, wincing as the tumble jarred her stomach and groin, which were both sore from the vigorous round of sex she'd just had.

"Shit," the man muttered, still holding one of her books. "I'm just making it worse, aren't I?"

His tone was self-deprecating and very dry. It made her want to smile.

But she was still sprawled on the floor with her tunic completely askew in front of a Combatant.

Combatants had plenty of status during the weeks of the Tournament every year, and the longer they lasted, the more money they earned.

She certainly would be happy to win the attention of any of them, although they'd never be her highest goal since their presence in the Residence was only temporary.

They all eventually left to go elsewhere, so they could never make her a long-term favorite and as safe and secure as Jenelle was.

They were also all young, strong, and fawned over, so they had their pick of sexual partners who didn't come with all the restrictions of the leisure suite.

He reached out an arm to help her to her feet, and she noticed when his gaze moved lower than her face. His eyes were a very dark blue. She could see now that he was closer. She'd never seen eyes that color, and she wondered if they were natural.

When she managed to stand up, she glanced down at herself and saw what had distracted him. Her torn tunic wasn't just askew. It was hanging partly open, revealing the swell of one of her breasts.

She found it kind of sweet that he kept trying to focus his eyes on her face, as if he weren't supposed to be looking. She gave him a little smile as she asked, "Do you always wear that mask, even when you're alone in your room?"

He blinked behind the eyeholes of the mask. "Oh. No. I put it on before I opened the door. It sounded like someone had knocked, and I didn't know who it was."

She nodded, wondering why it even mattered. Combatants were supposed to wear their masks at all times when fighting or attending public functions—one of the archaic rules of the sport that served no logical purpose now—but none of the others did so in domestic quarters or when simply hanging out around the Residence.

"I'm sorry to disturb you," she said, extending her hand for the book he still held. "I was just being clumsy."

He studied the book before he handed it to her. "Do you read all these books?"

"Why else would I have them?"

"I have no idea. I didn't think anyone read books anymore."

"I like the feel of the pages," she told him. "And the smell of them. I used to—" She cut herself off before she told him of the old man in her home village with the shelf of books. Her memories were one of the few things she could keep private, and there was no reason to share one with a stranger.

His eyes had slipped down to her chest again. He was definitely having trouble not looking.

"You used to what?" he asked, his voice revealing that his eyes weren't the only parts of his body affected by the glimpse of her breasts.

Never one to miss an opportunity—even if it was only a temporary one—she untied her sash and opened her tunic fully so he could see her, exactly as she had with the subcommander earlier.

It had worked before. Maybe today was her lucky day.

The man made a weird sound in his throat and turned away in a jerky move, gripping his doorframe tightly as he showed his back to her.

Talia grew still. "What's the matter?"

"Why are you doing that?" His voice sounded very stretched, and his shoulders were visibly tense.

Confused and strangely upset by his reaction to her innocent gesture, she asked, "You know what the ponytail means, don't you?"

"Yes. I know."

"Then why are you acting that way? You're allowed to look at me. You're allowed to touch me if you want."

"And you... want that?" The man was still refusing to turn around, and the knuckles of his fingers gripping the doorframe were whitening.

She was starting to feel a little better. He wasn't insulting her. He was new to the Residence and probably to this part of the world. Perhaps he didn't know all the policies regarding leisure escorts. Most men learned them right away so they could take advantage of what they offered, but maybe this man hadn't. "I wouldn't have opened my tunic had I not wanted to make myself available to you."

The man turned around, and she saw his eyes run up and down her body almost hungrily.

She hadn't been wrong. He did like the looks of her. In fact, he liked it a lot.

The thin trousers he wore did little to hide the fact that he was getting aroused.

"So you would just... with me..."

"Of course. Why wouldn't I?"

"With anyone?" He was still holding on to the doorframe very tightly with one hand.

"No, not with anyone. I prefer not to have sex with women. It's just my choice. And there are some men I don't like the looks of. I get to decide who I make myself available to, and they get to decide if they want me. Has no one ever told you how it works?"

"I-I already knew about the leisure suite. I just didn't think... I'm a nobody."

"Of course you're not a nobody. You're a Combatant, and we're six weeks in." She searched his face, wishing he wasn't wearing the damned mask so she could read his expression better. "I saw you fight last night," she added.

"Did you?"

"It was amazing."

He appreciated her words. He was a man. Compliments like that nearly always worked.

"And it's as simple as that?"

"Yes, it's that simple." She was frowning at him now and deciding she might have been wrong to offer herself to him in the first place. "There's nothing shameful in what I do, if that's what you're implying. I work with my body, just like you do."

"I... I guess it feels a little different to me, but you're right. I'm the last person in any world who should judge anyone's choices. It's been a long time since I've been on Earth. I'm sorry."

Cultures were different on different planets, and some of them were very old-fashioned. She'd encountered both men and women who'd wanted to shame her before, and she was glad this man wasn't so archaic in his thinking.

He interested her, but her interest would soon fade if he was going to make her feel bad about herself.

"Are you angry with me?" the man asked after a pause.

She gave a little jerk, realizing she'd never responded to his apology. "No. No, of course not. The leisure suite is new to a lot of people. I can understand if it's a bit confusing."

"It's not really—" He cut himself off, as if he'd rethought whatever he'd first intended to say.

She didn't understand him at all, but she'd liked that he'd said sorry. "Thank you for the apology," she said.

"Least I could do." His eyes had drifted down again, but something changed in his posture. He took a step forward, staring down at her belly. "What happened to you?" he asked in a different tone.

She put an instinctive hand on her stomach and looked down at herself, noticing that her skin was raw and inflamed from being rubbed against the edge of the table so roughly. "Oh. It's nothing."

He was definitely frowning now behind the mask. "Did someone hurt you?" He reached out and took the torn fabric of her tunic in one of his hands.

His response and the sudden rough texture of his voice made her feel weird, self-conscious. "No. Of course not."

His hand moved down to her reddened belly, and it was clear he didn't believe her. "You've been injured."

"Would you stop it? I haven't been injured. It's just... the price of doing business."

His eyes flew up to her face, and she saw, even with the mask blocking his features, when he put the pieces together. "Oh."

"Yes. Oh."

"And you still want to... with me."

She found it so strange and inexplicable that he couldn't seem to say the word sex to her. She'd never met anyone like him. "Yes. If you want to."

It was quite obvious that he did want to. Even with the distraction of his concern for her injuries, he was visibly erect beneath his trousers. All the way erect.

He was very nice-sized too.

The hand that had been touching her belly drifted upward slightly, stopping just under her breast. He was breathing faster now, and his eyes were devouring her half-naked body.

She gently moved his hand up farther until he was cupping one of her breasts. "I told you that you could touch me," she murmured.

He shifted his hand slightly, tweaking her nipple with his palm, and she sucked in a breath as the tiny move sent a tingle of pleasure down to her pussy.

That was quite unexpected.

"Fuck, you're so beautiful," he said in a harsh whisper.

She felt another tingle of pleasure, and she realized it was from his words, from their obvious sincerity.

He really thought she was beautiful, and she liked that he did.

"So what are you waiting for?" she asked, trying an eyelash flutter that seemed to work on a lot of men.

He jerked his hand back like he'd been burned. "No," he mumbled, turning his head so he wasn't looking at her anymore. "No, I can't. I'm sorry. I can't... like this."

"Okay," she murmured, surprised and disappointed but trying not to show it. She closed her tunic and picked up the stack of books she'd set down on the floor of the hallway.

No one wanted her to make a scene just because she'd been so close to scoring another victory for the day only to lose it.

It happened.

It happened a lot.

It happened to her more than to other girls.

Her body type wasn't in style. And she was new to the suite. She didn't have all the skills that other women did. She needed more practice.

But how was she supposed to get practice if men kept turning her down—even a man who was obviously aroused by her?

"It's not that I don't... don't like you," the man said when she'd started to turn away from him.

She paused and looked back.

"I do. You're.... you're perfect. But sex is... personal to me."

She nodded, feeling a little better about the rejection. "You don't have to explain yourself to me," she said with a smile. Might as well end things on a good note. Maybe he'd change his mind later on.

"Why not?" he asked with a frown in his tone.

"Because this is my job."

"But you're also a person, aren't you?"

She blinked, staring at him for a long moment, her heart doing a very strange skipping thing. "Yes," she said at last, just a little breathless. "I am."

"What's your name?"

"Talia."

"Talia," he repeated softly. "I'm Desh."

She nodded to acknowledge his introduction. Then she turned and walked away with her stack of books, wondering why she felt so upended by his matter-of-fact comment about her being a person.

She knew in theory that she was a person. Of course she did.

But from a very early age, she'd also known that wasn't how men saw her.

She'd been fourteen when her breasts had really started to grow. She'd always been a pretty little girl—everyone had always told her that—but once she'd developed a figure, they'd started looking at her differently.

Her parents were dirt poor, working in the mines like everyone else on her home planet, and they'd had to use what they had available to provide for their family. She was one of those things.

When she was seventeen, they'd made plans to marry her off to the richest man in the village, a merchant in his fifties who'd been leering at her since she was fourteen.

They'd told her she was lucky that he had even noticed her, and she'd believed them. She'd wanted her own room with a nice bed and the pretty clothes he could give her.

Why on earth wouldn't she want that?

She'd never had a boyfriend. There were few young men in the village. Many of the boys who were raised there left the planet by the time they were sixteen, in search of something better than the barren existence on such an isolated, undeveloped part of the universe. A few of them would eventually come back if they couldn't make it in the outside world.

Her father had kept her away from even the few boys around. He'd protected her virginity as if it were a monetary treasure.

She'd grown up understanding it was.

But just before the engagement was finalized, her father had heard of a call for beautiful young women—virgins preferred—to interview for the leisure suite. He'd used every bit of their savings to take her to the one developed planet in their solar system to be interviewed by a bored Coalition official.

The man had looked at her naked, verified she was a virgin, and sent her to meet with an older woman in a private room.

The woman had grilled her for more than two hours about everything from favorite foods to her masturbation habits. (Those questions were easy—she'd never had an orgasm until they'd given her a vibrator in the leisure suite.)

She'd done exactly as her father had said and continually lied about her age.

In that part of the universe, record keeping was sketchy, and no one bothered to double-check the year she was born.

Women were supposed to be eighteen to enter the leisure suite. Talia had done it at seventeen, and it had been the best thing she'd ever done.

Her family was taken care of for the rest of their lives, and she was able to live in comfort for the rest of hers.

And all she had to do was have sex.

It wasn't really that different from what she'd expected when she was younger. Her body was the one thing she had of value, and so she had to use it.

She might not be great at sex yet, but she was getting better.

Eventually she would have a room of her own like Jenelle did. Privacy to read or rest or anything she wanted.

If the price she paid was bruises across the stomach from a man turning her over a table, then she wasn't about to complain. Men were like that. They took what they wanted.

She had the sudden image of Desh touching her breast so gently. She could almost feel again the tingles of pleasure in her pussy from the featherlight brush of his palm, so unexpected, so strange.

She shook her head, telling herself not to dwell on it since it didn't mean anything significant.

Desh had turned her down.

And if he changed his mind and took her to bed in the future, he'd end up like all the others. They looked different and acted different, but when they fucked, men were all the same.

They all took what they wanted.

It was the second thing Jenelle had told her when she'd first arrived in the leisure suite, overwhelmed and nervous and so excited about the new life she was starting here.

Don't overthink it. Men will always be men.

TWO

The following day, Talia went back to the library in the middle of the afternoon.

She didn't need any more books, but she was about to scream from all the giggling in the common area of the suite. Occasionally she was afraid the giggles were at her expense, although she had no proof of it. Other than Jenelle, she didn't really have any friends, and a few of the other escorts—like Breann—seemed to dislike her for reasons she didn't understand.

She wanted to be alone for a while, somewhere other than in her sleeping pod, and the library was the only place she could do that.

It occurred to her that she might see the subcommander again. Jenelle had said his name was Marshall, when Talia had told her friend about her encounter the night before.

He'd donated to the suite this morning, so he must have enjoyed fucking her.

Maybe he would want to do it again.

When she stepped into the library, she noticed she'd left the curtains closed around her window seat the day before. She usually left them open, but she'd probably been distracted.

Since no one else ever used the library, it must have been her.

Since she already had books to read, she went to sit down at one of the archive stations and scrolled through various news outlets. She'd started to concoct a new daydream last night about a rebellion to overthrow the Coalition—and she enjoyed her daydreams more if she had real details to use in plotting them out.

There were always news accounts of a variety of minor revolts on planets throughout the Coalition, and she searched for some of them so she could learn more specifics.

All those minor revolts were doomed to fail. Everyone knew it. They were too localized, and the Coalition forces were too strong. Most revolts were wiped out almost as soon as they started.

If Talia were part of one of them, she'd suggest they try to find other groups to join forces with. Nothing could ever happen without a united front.

So she read and fantasized herself as a character in one of the stories she liked to read, doing something brave and significant, making a difference.

Changing the world.

She had a very good time for about a half hour until she heard a voice from the doorway to the library. "Well, look who it is."

She turned toward the door to see her subcommander, Marshall, walking in with a grin on his face. "There's my chubby girl. You were looking for me, weren't you?"

She'd been so lost in daydreams that she'd completely forgotten about him. But he obviously liked the idea of her wanting to see him again, so she gave him a trembling smile. "I didn't know where I could find you since you didn't tell me your name."

"My name is Marshall, and you can find me in the barracks wing." He was close to her now, looming over her seat, and he frowned as he looked down at the monitor screen. "Why are you reading that rebel trash?"

She'd found a circulated pamphlet on a multiplanet revolt on a far edge of Coalition space, and she'd been reading it with interest.

Her heart jumped as she realized this might reflect very poorly on her. Escorts weren't supposed to be interested in anything anti-Coalition.

No one was supposed to be interested in such things.

She swallowed and searched her mind for some sort of innocuous excuse. "It's pretty bad, isn't it? I had a... an appointment with someone who was talking about it, and I like to be informed. So I was doing a little research. The whole thing makes me kind of sick."

Evidently, she'd played it exactly right. Marshall's features relaxed. "If you have a partner who tries to involve you in anything like that, you should report him and refuse to see him again."

She kept her eyes very wide, very innocent. "Do you think so? I'm so sorry if I was stupid. I'm still learning how to do things. I won't do it again."

Marshall smiled. "Don't worry about it. You don't need to be smart to be good at your job." He lifted her to her feet and then reached down to untie her tunic, pulling the fabric back to reveal her breasts. "There's those big tits I like so much."

She took a deep breath, causing her breasts to rise and fall. His face flushed slightly, and she could tell he'd completely forgotten about what she'd been reading.

"I'm glad you're here," he continued. "I kind of like a quick fuck in the middle of the afternoon, and I know you like it too."

She dropped her eyelashes. "I do. Do you want to go to the suite today?"

"No sense in wasting the time. The library is as good a place as any. Suck me off like you did yesterday, then I'll do a little something for you too."

She took off her tunic, letting him leer at her body, completely naked except for her thigh-high boots. Then she got down on her knees and freed his cock.

It was a pretty close repetition to the day before. He fucked her mouth first, and then he bent her over the same table, holding on to her ponytail as he pounded into her from behind.

Her stomach was still bruised from yesterday, so she kept trying to reposition since it really hurt to bend all the way over. After a few minutes, she figured out that if she arched her back and pushed herself up with her arms, the table hit her at a different place on her abdomen and so didn't hurt her bruises.

She had to arch her back a lot to keep her bottom in the position Marshall wanted it, but she managed to make it seem like her repositioning was because she was feeling so good and not because she was uncomfortable.

And Marshall obviously liked that he could see her breasts shaking this way. He kept leaning over so he could see them and told her to get them "bouncing."

"Good girl," he grunted, slapping his pelvis against her ass hard and fast. "You've been waiting for this all day, haven't you?"

She babbled out how good she was feeling, how much she wanted him to fuck her this way.

She straightened her arms, bracing herself so she could shake her body more vigorously, her breasts bouncing so hard they made a slapping sound against her chest. She made whimpering sounds like she was coming and then kept it up to fake a second orgasm.

She almost groaned when he still wouldn't finish up since her thighs were tired and her back was hurting, but she bounced and jiggled and cried out loudly until he finally roared with his own climax, emptying himself into her with rough rolls of his hips.

"Oh yeah," he gasped from behind her, pulling out of her at last. When she fell forward onto the table, he rubbed her bottom, but then he surprised her by slapping it without warning. "How many times did you come for me today?"

She turned over since she didn't enjoy being spanked. She gave him a shy, downcast look. "Three."

"Tomorrow I'll get you to four."

She made a wordless sound of approval, but she was mentally cringing. Surely he wasn't going to trying to one-up himself every day.

These fucking sessions would end up lasting forever.

"You're the best fuck I've had in a long time," he said, reaching over to play with her ponytail.

"Thank you," she whispered, not having to pretend to be thrilled by those words. "You're the best I've ever had."

In terms of the sex itself, she would prefer one of the old men she usually got, who didn't have very much energy and so didn't demand much from her. But she couldn't ask for anything better than a subcommander of Special Forces, especially when he thought she was the best fuck he'd had recently.

She would bounce her breasts for as long as he wanted if it meant he would keep donating to the suite.

"Okay," he said, straightening up and tucking his cock back into his trousers. "I don't have time for anything more for you. But I like this kind of midafternoon break. We'll definitely do it again."

She promised to be here tomorrow and waited until he left. Then she leaned over to pick up her tunic, groaning out loud as her back stretched painfully.

She was going to end up with new bruises tomorrow.

She'd slid her tunic over her shoulders when a rustle near the window caught her attention.

It was the curtain by the same window seat she always used.

The curtains were closed instead of opened the way she normally left them.

And one of the curtains had moved. She was sure of it.

Frowning, she walked over and yanked it back to see that someone was sitting in the window seat with a book in his lap.

That Combatant she'd met the day before.

Desh.

He must have been here the whole time.

She made a strangled sound and stepped back quickly. "What are you doing here?"

"I didn't—I didn't—" He was flushed and moved awkwardly as he tried to stand up. He wasn't wearing his mask, but she saw it lying on the window seat. "I was trapped," he managed to say.

"You were watching us fuck?" She turned to look toward the table and recognized that this vantage point would have a perfect view. She'd been bent over the table, her back arched, her whole body shaking wildly as Marshall had fucked her from behind.

She'd had no idea someone else was watching.

"No!" Desh looked as horrified as she felt. "I told you. I was trapped. I was reading in the window seat when you came in."

"Why didn't you say something?"

"I didn't know you were even here until he came in. And then you'd already taken your clothes off, and then he was—" Desh covered his face with his hands.

He was handsome. Very handsome without his mask on. Younger than she'd expected with strong, classic features and high cheekbones. His eyes were even bluer than she remembered from the day before.

He was handsome and young and clearly mortified by the situation.

"I was trapped," he said again, staring down at the floor. "I had no idea you'd even come in, and then it was too late. I'm really sorry."

She was about to say he should be sorry and that he should have somehow let them know he was present, when she recalled herself.

There was no reason for her to be embarrassed. She'd just been doing her job. And Desh was obviously telling her the truth when he said that he'd ended up in the situation by accident and then hadn't known what to do.

She might have done the same rather than call attention to herself when someone was naked and the other person had his cock out.

Plus Desh was still a possible partner for her, and she'd be stupid if she made him feel even worse by being outraged.

"It's okay," she said with a sigh, after she'd come to this series of conclusions. "You didn't mean to."

His expression changed sharply, and he peered at her. "I honestly didn't mean to. But I thought you were angry about it."

"I'm not angry. I was... I was surprised." She gave him a little smile. "It's really fine. Sex isn't a big deal. That's the whole point of the leisure suite. We're not supposed to make a big deal about. I was just surprised. Some people actually like to fuck in public."

"You're obviously not one of them." He seemed to be relaxing, although he was still looking at her suspiciously, as if the fact that she was letting him off the hook was somehow dubious. "You can be mad at me if you want. I deserve it."

"No, you don't. It was an accident." She smoothed her ponytail and realized her tunic was still hanging open.

Desh had obviously started to notice this too since his eyes had drifted down and didn't immediately come back up to her face. "You're still bruised," he murmured, his voice thicker than before.

She checked his pants and saw that he was visibly aroused. Already. Even if her body wasn't currently in fashion, he obviously liked how it looked. "They don't heal overnight. You should know. There's nothing the med unit can do about bruises."

"That guy didn't seem to care if he was hurting you."

"He wasn't hurting me."

"You weren't liking it as much as you pretended."

She sucked in a breath. "That's none of your business. And how could you possibly know?"

"Your expression slipped sometimes," he said, his eyes moving between her breasts and her face.

She cursed herself inwardly. She really needed more practice if Desh had been able to see that. Hopefully Marshall hadn't noticed the slips as well.

"Not that that guy would notice. He was in some fantasy world where he was giving you what you wanted." Desh snarled. "Selfish bastard."

"He's not a bastard. He's a decent man and a soldier, and he wasn't hurting me. Sex is just sex."

Her thighs and back were so sore that she leaned against the table, and she was pleased when Desh stepped closer to her.

Maybe this would end up being a good thing, as awkward as it felt.

Maybe seeing her having sex proved to him what he was missing.

Maybe Desh would decide that he wanted her after all.

"You sound very matter-of-fact about it," Desh said, lifting his eyes to her face.

"Why wouldn't I be?"

"I don't know."

"You said sex was personal to you. I guess it makes sense that you wouldn't understand that it's not me. It's just something that I do. And I like for the men I do it with to enjoy it." His eyes had drifted down to her body again, so she took a risk. "I would make sure you would enjoy it too."

His whole body tightened, and his eyes jerked up to meet hers. "You're still trying to come on to me, after I just..."

"You said it was an accident."

"It was."

"Then why would I hold it against you?"

He moved his hand like he would touch her, but he stopped halfway. Smiling, she took his hand and moved it to her breast, the way she had the day before.

He cupped her breast very lightly, as if he were testing its weight. Then he moved his other hand up too and brushed both her nipples with his fingertips.

She felt that same tingle of pleasure, and she sucked in a breath in response to it. As he continued fondling her gently, it felt so good that she found herself trying to push her breasts into his hands.

"You're sure he wasn't hurting you?" Desh asked thickly. With one hand, he caressed down to her belly, and with the other he lightly twirled her nipple. "He looked... rough."

Her breathing was accelerating, and her pussy was starting to throb. She couldn't believe this was happening—her body reacting like this. "No. He didn't hurt me. He was a little rough, but I was agreeable." She paused. "You don't have to be so uncomfortable about it. Have you never seen anyone fucking before?"

"Yes. I have. But this was different." He didn't explain why it was different, and she couldn't help but wonder why it was different to him.

He took her breasts in both hands and circled the nipples with his thumbs, causing her to arch back and drop her head with a little moan.

"Shit," he breathed. "You're so incredibly sexy."

"Thank you."

He slid one hand up her neck, his gentle touch triggering all kinds of delicious nerve endings. Then he stroked her cheek and rubbed the line of her lips with his thumb.

She felt like she was melting, like she was made of butter. She moaned again and tried to suck his thumb into her mouth as if she were sucking his cock.

He was staring hotly at his thumb in her mouth when she realized what she was doing.

She was doing it for her, because she liked the way it felt.

When she was supposed to be doing things for him.

She usually was able to focus better than this. She wasn't sure why she was feeling this way at all.

She let his thumb slip out of her mouth and reached out to trail her hand down his chest toward his abdomen, very slowly. "They say there used to be a planet where there were orgy banquets every night. People would go there for vacations, and everyone would have sex."

Desh gave a little huff. "There was a planet like that. I've met someone who lived there."

"Really? I thought maybe it was just stories."

"No. It was real."

"What happened to the planet?"

"It died. Like a lot of things in this universe."

There was something poignant about the words. She wasn't even sure why. "Did you visit the planet yourself?"

"No."

"Then when have you seen people fucking before?" she asked, hoping he couldn't hear how she was panting.

He was teasing her breasts again, tweaking the nipples and then letting his fingertips run up and down the curves. "I spent a few years on an undeveloped planet. A really undeveloped one. I lived with a tribe who all slept in a cave.

They didn't have any qualms about having sex in front of other people."

"So why are you so embarrassed?"

"I'm not embarrassed."

"Yes, you are." Her hand had descended to the front of his trousers, and she brushed against the bulge there. "Did you get turned on watching me earlier? Is that why you're embarrassed?"

"No."

"You didn't get turned on?" She massaged his erection more purposefully.

He groaned helplessly and moved her hand back to the table she was propped against. "Yes, you turn me on. You make me absolutely crazy. Is that what you want to hear?"

"I know I turn you on. I just don't understand why you think it's wrong to take me the way you want to."

"I—" He didn't finish the sentence, but he started to caress her breasts again, more focused now, like he couldn't help himself.

She gasped at the surge of pleasure and dropped her head back again, stunned that she was so hot and wet and aching from such a gentle touch. "Oh fuck," she whispered as her whole body pulsed in pleasure and need. "Oh fuck, that feels so good!"

Desh's face was deeply flushed, a sheen of perspiration on his skin. He was breathing just as fast as she was. "Are you faking this?"

Her whole body jerked at the question. "What?"

Desh blinked. "I asked if you were faking this, like you were faking with that guy earlier."

All her arousal transformed into something cold and small and hurt. She wasn't even sure why. She just felt... used in a way she wasn't used to.

She pulled away from him, tying her robe and turning her back to him.

"Talia," he said thickly. "I didn't mean—"

"It doesn't matter what you meant," she said hoarsely.

She felt like she was about to cry, and she didn't even know why. There was no reason for her to react this way. He'd just asked her a question.

She was the one who had told him that sex wasn't a big deal.

It wasn't supposed to be a big deal in Coalition space. It was supposed to be easy and casual and meaningless, a way to relax and release tension. They even frowned on old-fashioned marriage. Nothing that would give people ideals or romanticized notions of the world.

Desh asking if she was faking was a perfectly legitimate question and not one that should bother her.

But it did.

A lot.

She couldn't stay here any longer. She ducked her head and left the library.

Desh was very aroused, and she guessed he wouldn't be able to rush after her. Not right away anyway.

She was right. She made it back to the leisure suite and then to her room, where she closed herself in her pod, trying to figure out why Desh's question had hurt her so much.

Sex wasn't supposed to be personal.

Nothing any man said to her should hurt.

But she hadn't been faking with Desh.

She hadn't been faking at all.

~

She wasn't sure how much time had passed before she heard someone banging on her pod.

She released the door and frowned when she saw Breann, who shared the room with her, grinning. "What?" Talia demanded.

"Someone is here to see you. A man."

"Really?" She perked up a little, wondering if it was someone wanting an appointment specifically with her. It didn't usually happen, but Marshall had been interested.

Maybe her luck was changing.

"How did you manage to score a Combatant?" Breann asked.

"Oh."

Now she knew who it was, and she wasn't sure she wanted to talk to him. But it would be ridiculous to hold a grudge, and it was in her best interest to be nice to him.

A Combatant would be a good partner. It would be good for her.

And she wasn't in the position to turn down a reasonable offer.

She needed to approach this like business. That was what Jenelle had always said. So she went to a mirror, smoothed down her ponytail, and then walked into the common room to find Desh standing near the door, looking a little stiff and wearing his mask.

He wore that damned thing all the time.

"Did you want something?" she asked as she approached him. She knew Breann and some other girls were trying to eavesdrop on the conversation, so she tried to keep her voice low.

So did Desh as he responded, "I wanted to apologize. You ran away before I could."

"You don't have to apologize."

"Yes, I do. I hurt you."

"No, you didn't." She managed to sustain a smile even though this conversation was making her uncomfortable.

"Yes, I did." He was frowning at her from behind his mask. "Why do you insist on arguing with everything I say?"

"Because what you're saying isn't right. I told you that you didn't hurt me."

"Then why did you run away?"

"I didn't. I just returned to my room."

His eyes were peering at her face so intently that she dropped her eyes to hide her expression. "I'm sorry," he murmured very softly. "I'm not very good with women."

Her eyes darted back up to his face.

"You can probably tell," he went on with a rueful smile. "I... I haven't been around women in a long time. I've been training for years on Mel Tana with The Master."

"You have?" she asked, genuinely interested by this piece of news. No wonder he was such a good fighter. Mel Tana was known throughout the universe as the best place to learn hand-to-hand combat skills, but very few people could last long with the strict discipline required of students.

Few comforts. Limited diet. No sex of any kind, not even self-pleasure.

The rigor and discipline were supposed to channel one's energy into physical prowess.

"Yeah," Desh admitted. "I'm embarrassingly out of practice in talking to women, and I was never very good at it to begin with. I didn't mean to hurt your feelings."

"That's okay," she said, relaxing for the first time as she finally started to understand him. If he'd been on Mel Tana for years, then that meant he hadn't had sex in years. No wonder he seemed so inexperienced. "I understand."

"It's not because I don't like you. It's because I do."

She felt tingles of pleasure down her spine again, and she felt her cheeks flushing. "You do?"

"Yeah."

She wished he wasn't wearing that stupid mask so she could read his expression better. "I can... I could meet you tonight if you want me to. You could just stop by here when you want. I don't have any other appointments."

He stared at her for long time, his eyes sober behind the mask. Then he finally said, "You want to?"

"Yes. I do." Of course she did. And not just because he was a Combatant and a potential partner.

"Can you come to my room instead?"

"Yes. Yes, I can."

"Okay. I'd like you to."

This admission seemed to make him self-conscious, and he left almost immediately.

Talia didn't care though. Her heart was racing with excitement, and she was smiling as she turned around.

"Look who's the dark horse," Breann said as he passed.

Talia just gave her a cool smile.

She'd fucked a subcommander earlier, and now she had an appointment with a Combatant.

Both were good for her position in the leisure suite, but Desh was a lot more exciting to her personally.

She'd never felt this way before—not about sex.

But the truth was she couldn't wait to get to his bedroom tonight.

THREE

Talia stopped by Jenelle's room before she left the leisure suite that evening.

"When does he arrive?" Jenelle asked after she'd given Talia's appearance her approval. She wore her best tunic and had taken care with her makeup. Her hair and boots were always the same.

"I'm going to his room."

"Why?"

"I don't know. He said he'd prefer that."

Jenelle started to frown, which made Talia decidedly nervous.

"Is that wrong?" Talia asked, smoothing back her hair although it already looked perfect, with no flyaways or bumps. "I've done it before with other guests. Should I not have agreed to go to his room?"

"No. Of course you can go to his room. I'm just wondering why he wouldn't come here." She paused. "It's usually only older men who want to stay in their rooms. Was he embarrassed?"

"I don't know. Maybe." Talia tried to remember Desh's expression during their conversation earlier in the afternoon, but he'd been wearing that stupid mask and so he'd been difficult to read. "I couldn't really tell. He just asked, and I said yes."

She was starting to experience a familiar helplessness— one that reminded her that she was still new to this and didn't always make the best decisions.

She'd been so excited about meeting Desh, but maybe she shouldn't have been.

When Jenelle didn't respond, Talia added, "I think this might be his first time on Earth, and he's... not comfortable in this culture yet. Do you think it's a bad sign that he wouldn't come to the suite?"

"Not necessarily. I've just found that men who are ashamed of what they do with us will sometimes not treat us well. So just be careful."

Talia sat down on a soft, rounded footstool, her shoulders drooping. "I will. But I don't think he's going to treat me bad. He doesn't seem like that. He seems... gentle."

Jenelle gave her a sudden, sharp look. "Don't ever romanticize, Talia."

"I'm not!"

"Aren't you?"

"No. I... I like him, and I think he seems... not as hard as most of the men I meet. But I'm not romanticizing. I promise."

Jenelle relaxed slightly, but her eyes were still observant. "All right. Just please be careful. If you find a partner you like, then that's good. If you enjoy being with him, then that's good too. But as soon as you start getting foolish dreams or impossible ideas about him, that's when you'll run into danger."

"I know that. I'm not going to forget. I promise I'm not romanticizing. I really do think he's new to this sort of thing. He's never been with an escort before. He told me that sex is... is personal to him."

"Talia, you're not going to be personal to him, no matter what he says," Jenelle said. "You'll never be personal. Remember who you are to him."

"I know. I know! I was just explaining why he might have wanted me to come to his room. Do you... do you think I shouldn't go at all?"

"I'm not saying that. He's a Combatant, so that's a good thing. If you don't have any negative vibes about him, then you're probably fine. Just be careful. If a man feels bad or guilty about what he's doing, then he'll often take it out on you. If you get any sign of that at all, you get out of that room. If you can't get out, then you sound the alarm. No donation is worth being hurt for."

Talia nodded soberly, a shuddering beginning in her chest that she hadn't felt in a long time, not since her first month working here.

It had never once occurred to her that she should worry about Desh, that he could hurt her, but she was starting to get nervous now.

What if she was wrong about him?

What if she'd been as foolish as Jenelle feared?

Jenelle seemed to recognize her change of mood because her expression softened. "I didn't mean to bring you down, Talia. I just want you to be careful. Remember, men will always be men. They'll never be who you want them to be."

"I know," Talia said with a little smile. "I'm not going to forget."

~

Her excitement about her evening with Desh had transformed completely, and she felt chilled and shaky as she walked the long corridors of the Residence to the wing where Desh's room was located.

She almost wished she hadn't stopped by to talk to Jenelle first.

But it was better to be smart and subdued than to be foolish and happy.

Foolish happiness would only get her hurt.

She stood for a minute in front of his door, breathing deeply and trying to still her trembling hands. Then she buzzed, and he opened the door after just a moment.

He was dressed in his normal light trousers and top, and he wasn't wearing shoes or a mask.

He had dark bristles on his jaw from a day's worth of beard, and his face looked young, very attractive.

She sucked in a breath.

"Hi," he said with a little smile, dropping his eyes and then lifting them again.

"Hi." She clenched her hands when they started shaking again.

Surely he wouldn't transform into someone else.

Surely he wouldn't hurt her.

He looked quiet. And a little uncertain.

"Come on in." He stepped aside to let her in.

His room was like most of the regular guest chambers in the Residence, clean and comfortable and decorated in a sleek, minimalistic style.

"Do you want something to drink?" Desh asked, shifting his weight from foot to foot very subtly. "Some fake wine?" He gestured at the replicator in the wall.

"Are you having anything?"

He shook his head. "I've spent too many years only eating and drinking real food. I can barely even swallow down replicated stuff now."

He'd been on Mel Tana for years, she remembered. No replicators were even allowed on that planet.

"Do you want something to drink?" he asked again.

She shook her head mutely. She didn't want to drink anything if he wasn't. When she was with a man in the evenings, she had a few practiced routines she used to move into sex. But none of them felt appropriate right now, and she was still shaky and trying to hide it.

The only seats in the room were a couple of metal chairs, so she went to sit down on the edge of the bed, crossing her arms in front of her stomach in an attempt to stop her trembling.

Desh came to sit down beside her.

Someone needed to say something, so she said, "They do have real wine in the Residence."

"I know. But I haven't had real alcohol in so long that it would completely knock me out. I've got to fight tomorrow."

She nodded, staring down at the floor, trying not to imagine the sweet man beside her turning into some sort of monster during sex. He was strong. Really strong.

He could hurt her if he wanted to.

She took a slightly shaky breath. "What do you drink then, if you don't drink wine or replicated stuff?"

"Water. Or milk. Although the milk here is so processed I—" He cut himself off.

She turned her head to check his expression. "What?"

He slanted her a rueful smile before he glanced away again. "I just realized I sound like I'm complaining about everything."

"No, you don't. I've never heard of anyone who stayed on Mel Tana for so long. It must be strange to come back to the real world."

He gave a strange, soft huff. "The real world. Yeah."

He sounded almost bitter, and she didn't know why.

She tightened her arms around her belly and searched her mind for something to say, something to do, some way to stop shaking.

"Talia?"

She was staring at the floor. It felt safer that way. "Yes?"

"Why are you scared?"

"I'm not—"

"Yes, you are. Are you scared of... of me?"

She was blowing this. She was ruining it. What should have been a great thing for her was turning into a complete mess. She straightened her shoulders and tried to smile. "Of course not."

Desh reached over and took both her hands. His were big and warm and very strong. "You're shaking."

"I'm..."

"You're scared."

She let out a breath and met his eyes, so trapped there was nothing she could say. "I'm sorry."

His eyebrows had drawn together. "Don't be sorry. Just tell me why you're scared."

"I talked to my... my friend before I came here. She said that sometimes men will want to stay in their rooms if they're... they're ashamed of what they're doing. And that sometimes that shame will lead them to... hurt us."

She shouldn't have told him that. It was exactly the wrong thing to say.

If he were what Jenelle had feared he was, it would only make him angry.

But maybe it was better to find out now.

Desh's face twisted. "You think I'm going to hurt you?"

"No. No." She looked down to the floor again. "I don't know." She swallowed hard and pulled her hands out of his grip. "I thought I was getting better at this, but I guess I still don't know what I'm doing."

Desh was quiet for a long time. Then he murmured, "I don't know either."

He meant it.

He was as uncertain as she was.

It was the best thing he could have said to her. It immediately relieved her trembling nerves.

He was exactly who she'd thought he was. She hadn't been wrong about him.

No matter their respective positions, she had as much power in this room as he did.

She turned her head and slanted him a little smile. "Not very sexy, am I?"

His eyes widened as the rest of his expression relaxed. "You didn't just say that, did you?"

"Yes. Why?"

"Because you're the sexiest thing I've ever seen."

Her heart started to hammer again but not with nerves this time. "Even now?"

He reached out to brush his fingers along her cheek and then down the line of her neck. "Especially now."

The light touch felt so good she sucked in a breath. "You still want to do this?"

"Do you?"

She nodded.

"Then I do too."

She stood up, untied her tunic, and let it slip off her shoulders.

The response in Desh's face and body was immediate, dramatic. His eyes went hot. His body went tight. He stared up at her speechlessly.

Then he reached to pull her down so she was sitting beside him again. He cupped one of her breasts the way he had before, his touch so light it was almost delicate.

She liked the faint flush on his cheeks, the way his breathing had sped up, the way his hand shook just slightly. It was proof that he was really liking how she looked, how she felt.

It made her feel special, and she wasn't used to feeling that way.

She hadn't been wrong about him.

At all.

This was a good decision.

"How do you want to do this?" he asked in a thick voice.

"We can do anything you want."

At the moment, he seemed to want to touch her. He took her breasts in both hands and twirled her nipples until she couldn't help but let out a soft, lingering moan.

"Do you like how that feels?" he asked, trailing his hands down to her waist and then her hips.

"Yes," she whispered.

When his hands went back up to her breasts, she arched her back, trembling again but not from fear now.

Her pussy was already pulsing with arousal. She had no idea how it was even happening.

Remembering that she was supposed to be making him feel good, she said, "I can touch you if you want."

"I want to touch you first. Can you lie down for me?"

She could hardly argue with him, but she was feeling more and more out of control. She adjusted her position so she was stretched out on the bed on her back, and he'd moved over her, his eyes raking hungrily over her body, which was naked except for her boots.

She gasped when he let his fingertips trail from her breasts to her thighs. Then she gasped again when he teased one of her nipples with his thumb.

She tried to catch her breath.

She shifted her hips restlessly.

"Fuck, you're so beautiful. Can I…?" He didn't finish his question.

"You can do anything you want," she told him in a breathless whisper.

He leaned over and took one of her breasts in his mouth.

She made a little whimper and arched up at the jolt of pleasure.

"Are you okay?" he asked, lifting his head to look at her face.

"Yes."

"What's the matter?"

"I'm not used to feeling this way," she admitted, clenching her fingers into the soft coverlet.

"What way?"

"Good."

His expression changed as he processed her words. A different kind of heat flared from his blue eyes.

He leaned back down to suckle her nipple until she was squirming helplessly.

Then he straightened up and slid one hand down between her legs. Before he touched her pussy, he asked, "Can I?"

She nodded, completely incapable of speech at the moment.

His fingers explored just as gently as he'd touched her everywhere else. Almost hesitant. When he slid one finger inside her, she clenched around it eagerly.

His lips parted slightly, his cheeks more flushed than before. "You're so wet."

She was wet. She'd never been so aroused in her life, and she was almost embarrassed by it, like it wasn't a professional way to behave.

There was no way she could help it though.

Her body desperately wanted what he was doing to her.

"Do you... do you like this?" he asked, moving his eyes from her pussy to her face.

She nodded and fisted her hands in the coverlet.

He pumped his finger a few times, and she bent up her knees.

"Can you..." She bit down on her lower lip as the pleasure intensified. "Can you use two fingers?"

He adjusted his hand so he was penetrating her with two fingers, and he slid them in and out of her, creating delicious friction.

She wasn't supposed to be doing this.

She wasn't supposed to be letting him please her.

She was supposed to be pleasing him.

But she was too far gone now to make things right. She clutched at the bedding and rocked her hips against his fingers, tossing her head helplessly as the pleasure built up inside her.

"Faster," she gasped, squeezing her eyes shut and holding on for dear life. "Please!"

He accelerated his rhythm so he was fucking her hard with his hand, and the pressure at her center shattered into waves of sensation.

She bit her lip hard to stifle her cry of pleasure as she shook and shuddered.

Her whole body was hot and relaxed when he pulled his fingers out of her tight, wet pussy.

She was even wetter now than before. She'd soaked his hand.

Panting and still clutching at the coverlet, she couldn't even move for a minute. When she opened her eyes, she saw that Desh was still staring at her with that hot intensity.

"Why did you do that?" she managed to ask, feeling embarrassed and self-conscious by the way she'd lost control.

"Because you said I could do anything I wanted."

It was a strange sort of answer, but it told her something about him. Proved yet again that she hadn't been wrong in her first impressions of him.

Wanting to show that she appreciated what he'd done, she sat up and moved onto her knees, easing him down so he was lounging against the pillows. "Can I do something for you now?" she asked with a little smile.

His whole body clenched visibly. "Yes. Please."

She slowly took off his clothes, very pleased by the sight of his firm body beneath them—all long limbs and lean, well-defined muscles. He was utterly silent as she caressed his shoulders, his arms, his chest, his legs. His cock had been fully erect from the time she took off his trousers, and it was resting up against his belly, waiting for her to touch it.

She finally did, causing Desh to jerk slightly and suck in a loud breath.

Her heart was racing as she lowered her mouth, and he groaned long and low as she teased him with her tongue, twirling the head, licking a line down his shaft.

He bucked his hips up jerkily when she took him fully in her mouth, his hands moving restlessly over the coverlet, as if he didn't know what to do with them.

"Fuck," he gasped when she started to suck. His upper body arched up off the bed. "Oh, fuck! I can't... I can't..."

She was strangely thrilled by his naked pleasure, his complete lack of control. She applied rhythmic suction and moved a hand under her head so she could gently massage his balls.

He arched up again, fumbling for purchase on the bed. He was making helpless little thrusts into her mouth, and she realized he was already about to come.

After a few more sucks and squeezes, he did come, letting out a loud groan that lasted for a long time. His cock shuddered in her mouth, and his body rode out the spasms until he was limp and panting and relaxed.

She swallowed down his release and let him slip out of her mouth as she straightened up. She was smiling like an idiot as she saw his sated expression and the flush all the way down his neck.

She stroked his chest gently until he'd recovered enough to meet her eyes.

"Well, that was embarrassing," he muttered.

She frowned. "Why?"

"I lasted about two seconds."

She giggled as she massaged his shoulders. "You lasted longer than that. And what does it matter?"

"I thought we might do something else," he said, slightly sheepish.

She couldn't seem to stop smiling, and she didn't even know why. "We can. I imagine it won't be long until you're up for more."

He was smiling too as he pulled her down to lie beside him. She wasn't exactly sure what he wanted, but she fit herself at his side and used one hand to stroke his chest.

She kind of liked that he wasn't completely hairless. It was unusual, and she couldn't help but play with the hair on his chest.

He had one of his arms around her, but it was only holding her loosely. His body was still warm and soft from his release.

"Do you like doing that?" he asked after a few minutes.

She was surprised by the question and raised her head to see his face. "What do you mean?"

"I mean, do you like doing that?"

She blinked, unsure of how to answer.

"You can tell me the truth," he said quietly, his eyes sober on her face. "I'd rather you not make up pretty lies to please me."

"I wasn't going to lie," she told him. "I was just... thinking it through. Sometimes I don't like it. Sometimes it feels... uncomfortable. But most of the times I'm focusing on how to do a good job." She paused. "I like to do good at my job, the same as anyone else."

He nodded, as if he understood. "You did a really good job with me."

She gave him a trembly little smile. "I liked it," she admitted. "With you. I don't know why, but I did."

"You don't have to tell me that, if it's not true."

"It is." She lay back down, embarrassed by the admission and not sure why she was making it. "It is true."

He stroked her hair and didn't say anything.

She continued to caress his chest, occasionally trailing her hand down to his tight belly. After a few minutes, she noticed that his cock was starting to harden again.

He was a lot younger than most of the men she'd been with.

It didn't take long.

She gave his abdomen little strokes and touches, oddly excited by the response she saw in his cock. She liked how it was hardening. She liked how it took so little for him to get aroused again.

Her hand got lower and lower until she heard him suck in his breath.

"You ready for something more?" she asked, trying to sound sophisticated and enticing rather than breathless.

"Yes," was all he said.

He gazed at her as she raised herself up to her knees, and his expression was breathtaking—hot and eager and almost awed.

It almost scared her—that look of awe in his eyes—but she didn't let it distract her.

Since he was still lounging against the pillows and obviously waiting for her to do something, she asked, "How do you want to do it?"

He gave his head a little shake. "You decide."

Men never let her decide the position they wanted. The fact that Desh had was strange and unsettling.

He hadn't yet moved though, so she figured he might want her on top. She caressed her way down his body and then moved to straddle his hips. "Do you like this?" she asked, trying to read his preferences in his expression.

His lips parted as he stared up at her, like he'd tried to speak but couldn't. He nodded.

She arranged herself above him and then reached down to fit his cock inside her. She was still wet and pliant from her earlier orgasm, so he slid into her pussy easily, filling her with a pleasurable tightness.

She wasn't used to enjoying how a man's cock felt inside her. She rolled her hips against the sensations and made a little moan.

Desh moaned too, his hands moving against the bedding the way they had when she'd had his cock in her mouth.

"Is this good for you?" she asked.

"Yes," he hissed, his hips rocking just slightly beneath her, as if he couldn't hold himself still but didn't want to thrust. "You feel so good."

He seemed so oddly passive that she started to worry. "Do you want to be on top? Do you like it better another way?"

He closed his eyes and arched his neck, his expression reflecting deep pleasure. "I like it this way," he rasped after a minute.

Convinced he was enjoying it, Talia started to move over him. She began slowly, rhythmically, using a number of her practiced techniques. Desh was still making those little rocks with his hips and was clenching his hands in the bedding the way she'd been doing earlier.

His eyes were open now, gazing up at her, and his expression was so disturbing that she could barely look at it. She didn't know how to understand it.

His motion felt almost helpless rather than controlled, but it had the strangest effect on her body. Combined with her own motion, pleasure was starting to tighten inside her.

She increased her speed, riding him more vigorously to meet the demands of her body. She was making soft, little grunts as she moved, but she couldn't possibly help it. Everything was feeling so good.

Desh must be enjoying it too because he was releasing choked moans and clutching desperately at the coverlet. He suddenly gave a few hard pushes up into her, and she cried out loudly in response.

"Yes!" she gasped. "Do that more. More. I need more!"

She wasn't supposed to make demands on a man in bed, but the words were spilling out of her lips. She was riding him almost frantically now, her whole body bouncing as she chased a release that was just out of reach.

Desh started to thrust up more intentionally, his cock pushing into her from below fast and hard.

She bent backward like a taut bow as she fell into orgasm, sobbing out a pleasure that was as shocking as it was deep.

Her pussy clamped down around his cock as she came, and his motion fell out of rhythm almost immediately. He reached up to hold on to her hips, his grip tight and urgent, and his whole body was rocking as he fucked her from below, his groans getting louder and more uncontrolled.

She had come down enough to watch him as he built up toward climax, and she couldn't help but love how raw and earnest he seemed, no pretense, no layers of fake sophistication.

He was completely into this, pouring everything he had into the motion of his body, the sensations he was experiencing.

She watched as the pleasure of release slammed into him, his face reflecting all of it. He let out a sound that was almost a bellow, holding nothing back as he rocked through his release in clumsy jerks.

When all the spasms had worked their way through him, he collapsed back onto the bed with thick, breathless groans, one right after the other.

Her own pussy was still making little clenches of lingering pleasure, and her whole body felt good, relaxed, strangely heavy.

She started to get off him, but he pulled her down onto his chest.

So she lay there gasping, his arms wrapped around her tightly.

It was several minutes before his body really relaxed and he finally released her.

She lifted her head to smile down on him.

"You came for real?" he asked, his eyes searching her face.

It was the last thing she'd expected him to ask, so she didn't have time to frame an answer. She just told him the truth. "Yes. It was real."

The corners of his mouth went up. "Good. For me too."

The last words were dry, ironic, and she giggled helplessly, moving to his side where it was more comfortable.

"It's been a long time for you, I guess," she said after a few minutes, following the line of her thoughts.

"What do you mean?" His body tightened, and she was momentarily afraid she'd offended him.

She replied quickly, "I just meant I know you've been on Mel Tana, and you can't have sex there. At least you're not supposed to. You didn't break the rules, did you?"

"No. I didn't break the rules."

"That's a long time to go without sex."

"Yes. It is." There was a strange, stretched tone to his voice that she didn't understand.

"Why did you go there? And why did you stay there so long?"

"I... I don't really know."

That sounded like a hedge, like a stall, so she didn't reply right away.

After a moment, he continued, "I told you I was on that primitive planet with the tribe that slept in the cave. I was there for three years, and it was... it was really hard coming back. Life was so raw and intense and... hard on that planet that I couldn't really adjust. Everything felt too... rich, too soft, too... fake. I felt sick all the time. So someone told me about Mel Tana and the rigorous nature of the training there, and I thought it would work as a transition, help me get used to the developed world again."

She was listening intently, fascinated by what he was telling her. "Did it work? As a transition, I mean."

He shook his head. "I don't think so. I... couldn't seem to leave."

"Did you even want to learn how to fight?"

"I've actually never been very physical. I was academic growing up. Pretty much a nerd, really. But I felt helpless on that planet, having to rely on stronger men for food, for protection. I didn't ever want to be that way again. So the training on Mel Tana helped. A lot. I never cared that much about fighting, but I wanted to be... strong. I don't ever want to feel helpless again."

"What made you leave Mel Tana at last then?"

He sighed and gave her a sheepish smile. "I... A couple of things happened. I got some... some really bad news that made it impossible for me to keep doing what I'd been doing. And then I got kicked out. The Master said I was hiding from the world and it was time to stop." After a pause, he added, "He was right."

She thought about this for a long time. "What was the bad news?"

He shook his head silently. He wasn't going to tell her.

They weren't that much more than strangers, after all.

Accepting this, she asked, "Are you glad you left?"

"I... I don't know yet." He ran his palm down her long ponytail. "But I can say that nothing on Mel Tana ever made me feel as good as you did just now."

She smiled at that. "So it has been a long time since you've had sex?"

"Y-yeah."

His tone was strange, so she lifted her head to study his face. "You had sex on that undeveloped planet? In the cave with everyone else?"

His mouth twisted strangely.

Her eyes widened as she realized what he didn't want to tell her. "Have you never had sex before, Desh?"

She saw him swallow. Then something relaxed on his face and he admitted, "No. This was my first time. I'm twenty-eight, and I was a virgin until tonight. Pitiful, isn't it?"

"No, it's not pitiful." She was surprised but also something else. Something that felt a lot like delight. She was the only woman he'd ever slept with. She couldn't help but like that fact. "One thing I've learned from my work here is that everyone has their own reasons for having sex or not having it. Some people just aren't that interested. Some people just don't want it."

He gave a huff of ironic amusement. "Oh, I was interested in it. I was *very* interested in it. I wanted to have sex every single day."

"Then why did you stay on Mel Tana?"

He shook his head and stared at the ceiling. It took him a long time to answer. "I wonder if part of me... wanted to deprive myself, like maybe I deserved it."

She stiffened. "Why would you possibly deserve to be deprived like that?"

It was too intimate a question, and she knew it as soon as she voiced it.

Desh's lips tightened, and he murmured, "I don't know."

He did know. He just didn't want to tell her.

And she had no right to know something so private anyway.

She relaxed beside him and gradually felt him relax too.

She really liked how sated his body felt beside her, like she'd given him a really good time.

She wanted to make him feel really good.

She wanted to keep making him feel good.

It just wasn't right that he hadn't been letting himself feel good for so long.

Maybe he would want her to help him make up for lost time.

She'd be very happy to oblige.

FOUR

The next evening was another round of the Tournament, and Talia didn't feel her normal reluctance about attending.

She wanted to see Desh fight.

She wanted to see him win another round.

She was absolutely sure that he would.

It was a strange feeling and one she couldn't remember ever experiencing before. Something akin to pride.

She didn't mention it to Jenelle as they took their seats in the leisure suite section. In fact, except for telling her friend that last night had gone well, she didn't talk about Desh at all.

But she felt restless and jittery as she looked around at the packed arena and waited for the fights to begin.

"What happened last night?" Jenelle asked out of the blue.

Talia stiffened her shoulders. "What do you mean?"

"You think I can't see how you're feeling? I told you not to romanticize. It's work, Talia. Nothing but business." Despite her words, Jenelle's voice wasn't sharp. It was almost gentle.

"I'm not romanticizing. I'm not doing anything at all."

Jenelle slanted her a dubious look.

"All right," Talia admitted with a sigh. "I'm feeling... I do like him. I... I enjoyed last night more than I've ever enjoyed being with a man. But I'm not being stupid. I promise. I thought it was all right to enjoy it."

"It is." Jenelle's expression was subdued, but she didn't continue the conversation. That fact alone was enough to make Talia worry.

She didn't have time to worry much, however, since the announcer was speaking and the Combatants were starting to enter the rings.

Five combat rings this week.

Talia waited breathlessly until she saw Desh walk out in his mask. The other Combatants were playing to the crowd—shaking their fists and raising their arms—but Desh didn't do any of that. He ignored the cheers and walked over quietly to take his place.

He looked almost small next to the monster of a man he had to fight tonight. For a moment Talia was worried.

Then she remembered he'd spent years on Mel Tana. He'd taken less than a minute to defeat his opponent last week.

He was better at this than anyone.

He would be fine.

As the Combatants waited in place for the buzzer to sound, Talia noticed Desh turning his head in her direction. From this distance, she couldn't imagine he could actually see her in the audience, but the move of his head seemed to acknowledge her, as if he were thinking of her.

She hugged her arms to her chest, trying to hide a shiver of pleasure.

"Damn," she heard Jenelle mutter under her breath.

Talia would have turned and asked about the soft curse, but the buzzer was sounding the beginning of the fights.

She was excited as the Combatants advanced, but her excitement soon transformed into something very different.

After the first couple of minutes, she was concerned. Desh didn't seem to be doing as well.

After another few minutes, she was cringing, her heart racing up in her throat. Desh's opponent was twice his size, and Desh couldn't seem to get a handle on him.

After a few minutes, Talia was hiding her eyes, peeking out from between her fingers and trying not to whimper.

Desh had gotten thrown bodily across the ring, and before he could get to his feet again, the big man had grabbed him in a ruthless hold that looked like it would break his back.

As Desh struggled futilely to free himself, Talia had to look away, closing her eyes and afraid she might be sick.

She was going to be sitting here while the man killed Desh. Combatants weren't supposed to kill their opponents, but it did happen occasionally.

There were no real rules or boundaries in these fights. Combatants could do what they needed to do to win.

"What's happening with him tonight?" Jenelle asked breathlessly. There were four other fights going on at the same time, but she was obviously focused on the same one Talia was. "He did so much better last week."

Talia tried to answer but couldn't. She'd glanced back over and almost choked as she saw the big man had forced Desh to the floor. She squeezed her eyes shut and prayed to any force in the universe that might hear her.

"He's got it," Jenelle said in a different voice. "He's gotten control of it again."

Talia breathed again as she opened her eyes to see that Desh had indeed regained his footing. She watched openmouthed as he evaded his opponent's reach once. And then again. And then again.

Then Desh managed to get behind him and, with some fancy footwork, kicked out at the other man with a sharp impact on the back of his neck.

The big man went down and didn't get back up.

Talia slumped in relief as the crowd roared in excitement.

Desh was hurt. She could see it in the way he stood, the way he walked.

But he'd won this round, so she could breathe easy again.

~

Two hours later, she went to Desh's room.

They hadn't made a firm appointment, but the way they'd ended the night before had made it clear Desh wanted to see her again. Even if he wasn't up to sex tonight after the fight, she needed to make sure he was all right.

When the door slid open and Desh wasn't in the doorway, she stepped in, looking around.

She gasped when she saw Desh sitting on one of the straight metal chairs.

She'd assumed he'd gone to get medical treatment for his injuries, but he clearly hadn't. He hadn't even washed up after the fight.

He still wore the trousers he'd worn to fight in and nothing else. Blood was drying on the side of his face and the back of his shoulders. He was leaning over, supporting his head with one hand on the table.

"Desh!" she cried, hurrying over. "What the hell are you doing?"

He didn't answer. Just stared at her with pained blue eyes.

"You're hurt! Why didn't you go to the med unit?"

He opened his mouth and then closed it again.

"Desh?"

He finally rasped, "I'm fine."

"No, you're not. You're bleeding. Let me take you to—
"

He pulled away from her hands with a slight wince. "I said I'm fine."

"Well, you're not fine." She stood and stared at him, anxious and confused. "You really won't go let them fix you up?"

"I don't need to be fixed up. There's nothing serious."

He didn't sound like himself. He sounded tense, clipped.

She was too worried to work out why though. She went to the sink in the nook with the bathroom and wetted down a soft cloth. When she returned to Desh, she started to wipe the blood off his face.

He leaned away from her. "You don't need to do that."

"Would you just shut up?" She was so rattled she sounded almost bad-tempered. It wasn't the right way to talk to a guest in the Residence, but she'd completely lost her patience with him. "If you're not going to go to the med unit, you're going to put up with me."

He started to object again. She saw it in his face. But then he stopped himself and sat still as she wiped the blood off his face.

He had several cuts, but the deepest was on his temple and just above one of his shoulder blades.

The skin was ripped too much for a cloth and bandage to do much good.

She looked up and saw that Desh's eyes were focused on her through the mirror over the table.

She shook her head at him. "You really won't go to the med unit?"

"I said I'm fine. I've been injured a lot worse than this, and there are no med units on Mel Tana."

She gave him a little scowl, fed up by his stubbornness, but then she saw him cringe as he shifted in his chair.

"Do you have any broken bones?"

He started to shake his head but then admitted, "A couple of cracked ribs maybe."

She made a frustrated noise in her throat. "Stay here. I'll be right back."

"What are you—"

"I said stay here."

When she left his room to hurry down the halls of the Residence, she felt the almost irresistible urge to wring his neck.

What kind of stupid, stubborn man would just sit there in pain when he could do something to feel better?

What the hell was wrong with Desh?

When she reached the med unit, she asked to borrow a handheld medical device—an all-purpose unit that could deal with most injuries—and on her way back to Desh's room, she felt less annoyed and more concerned.

Desh wasn't just being stubborn.

He'd almost lost the fight earlier when he shouldn't have.

Something really must be going on with him.

When he let her back into his room, he hadn't moved from the chair. She went over and started running the device over his body, starting with his head. It mended the torn skin in just a few seconds and then took longer to work on the cracked ribs.

It even had a setting to make a person unconscious. If Desh was too frustrating, she might be tempted to use it on him.

He was going to be covered with bruises, but even technology couldn't do much to fix that.

Desh sat in stiff silence as she worked over him, but she saw his posture change as his wounds were mended and the pain was relieved.

When she was done at last, she put the med device on the table and went to rinse out the cloth she'd been using earlier.

After rewetting it, she started rubbing it over his skin again, cleaning off the remaining blood and the dried sweat on his face and body.

She felt shaky and strangely tender as she cleaned him up.

When the silence became too deep, she said, "See? If you'd just gone to the med unit right away, you could have felt better in fifteen minutes instead of being in pain for hours."

His blue eyes held hers in the mirror. "The injuries weren't that bad," he said hoarsely.

"But they were still injuries. Why shouldn't you make them better?"

"I've had far worse before, on planets without med devices."

Her eyes widened. "So what? So just because you've suffered before, you have to suffer now?"

He broke her gaze, staring blindly at a spot across the room.

As her words lingered in the silence, she suddenly realized they were true.

They were entirely true.

Desh did feel like he was supposed to suffer.

Part of him even wanted it.

He'd spent years depriving himself of the most basic kinds of comforts, depriving himself of sex, of any sort of pleasure.

He *wanted* to suffer.

"Desh," she whispered, on the verge of tears. He was mostly clean now, and the physical pain was obviously gone, but he looked haunted, broken, lonely.

She reached out for him instinctively.

"Don't," he muttered, easing away from her hands.

She stared at him for a long time, trying to figure out what she should do, what she *could* do.

Finally she asked softly, "What happened in the fight this evening?"

He let out a breath and turned his head to meet her gaze again. He gave a very slight shrug. "I... I lost focus."

She didn't know what to say to that, so she just stood staring at him, shaking slightly.

After a minute, he went on, "I knew better, but I lost focus. My mind was on... something else."

She suddenly understood why he kept pulling away from her. "On me? Was it... my fault?"

"It wasn't your fault. It was my fault. I shouldn't have... let myself take what I wanted."

"What? You think because you had sex you somehow lost focus? That's crazy, Desh."

"It's not crazy, Talia. That's exactly what happened." He stood up and met her eyes evenly, looking strangely hard, strangely cool. "I knew better than to indulge myself, but I did it anyway. And I almost lost everything because of it."

She clenched her hands at her sides. "What do you mean you lost everything? You won the fight, and surely this Tournament isn't the most important thing anyway. What about *you*? What about what's good for you?"

"What's good for me is to do what I'm here for."

"And what's that?"

He kept looking at her but didn't answer.

"Desh?" she prompted. "What is it? What's so important about this stupid Tournament that it's worth suffering for, denying yourself everything for?"

"It's not the Tournament. That's not why I'm here."

"Then why are you here?"

He opened his mouth like he would answer, but then he seemed to recall himself. He jerked slightly and turned away from her.

Then he took a couple of steps away and sat down on the edge of the bed, suddenly looking very young, very vulnerable.

Talia was almost in tears, and she couldn't have explained why. She went over to the bed to sit beside him. "Desh, please talk to me. Why are you here, if it's not for the Tournament? What's more important than you being happy?"

He didn't reply. He didn't even look at her.

At the end of her patience, she reached out and turned his head so she could see his expression. "Desh, tell me. Why do you think you always need to suffer? Why won't you let yourself feel good?"

76

They stared at each other with a strange intensity, and then suddenly something broke inside Desh. She saw it happen. His features twisted briefly, and he made a rough sound in his throat.

Then he was leaning into her, taking her head in his hands.

He kissed her.

He kissed her so urgently that he pushed her down onto the bed.

She'd never been kissed before—not really and definitely not like this. Her job was sex, and kissing had never been part of it. But she kissed him back immediately, instinctively. There was no way she could stop herself. She tangled her fingers in his thick hair, still damp from sweat and the wet cloth she'd wiped his face and neck with. She opened her mouth as his tongue nudged at her lips, and she moaned as the kiss and the weight of his body generated all kinds of tingling pleasure.

Her tongue played with his as arousal tightened between her legs. He was hard against her. Already. She rocked up into his erection, loving that he was so eager for her, that it took so little to turn him on.

"Oh fuck, Talia," Desh breathed, finally breaking the kiss to nuzzle at the hollow of her neck. "What are you doing to me?"

The helpless question just made her even more needy, more excited. She arched up into his body, running her fingernails down his bare back. He was hot and damp and smelled like effort. He filled her senses.

He lifted up enough to fumble at her clothes until he'd untied her tunic. He stared down at her hotly for a moment before he lowered his face to one of her breasts. He teased it with his lips and tongue until she was crying out helplessly.

Then he moved to the other one, suckling until she couldn't hold still. She squirmed and moaned and clawed at his back.

When she couldn't take any more erotic torture, she undid his trousers and reached inside so she could find his cock. He gasped and jerked against her as she wrapped her hands around him.

"Talia," he rasped, closing his eyes. "What are you doing to me?"

It was the same question he'd asked before. He was rocking his hips slightly into her hands, but he wasn't making any further advances. A flicker of worry caused her to ask, "Do you... do you want this?"

"I want it more than anything." The admission seemed to be ripped out of him, and he finally opened his eyes. "I want you so much."

She groaned in relief and spread her legs farther to make room for him. She was very wet, very aroused, and she desperately needed to feel him inside her. She helped him align his erection at her entrance and then bent up her knees as he started to edge himself inside her.

"Oh fuck," he moaned as the penetration deepened. He was holding himself up on straightened arms above her, and his face was twisting in obvious pleasure.

She bent her knees up even more so she could feel him more deeply, and she dug her fingernails into the back of his neck. She rolled her hips, and he groaned again.

His responses were raw, helpless, uninhibited.

Utterly genuine.

She loved that she could make him feel so good.

He held himself tensely above her, not moving his hips, so she wrapped her legs high around his back and lowered her hands to his firm ass.

She rocked her hips up into him a few times until he started to thrust.

His motion was fast, urgent, uncontrolled, and it felt so good she arched her neck and cried out her pleasure. She moved with him, squeezing around him on every thrust.

"That's right," she heard herself panting after a minute. "Faster. Harder. Take me harder. Desh, please!"

The bed was attached to the wall, but they were shaking the mattress vigorously. She could hear their flesh slapping together, and the rawness of it intensified her pleasure.

Desh was grunting like an animal now, his eyes fierce as they gazed down at her. He'd finally let himself go, and all the passion and effort he'd controlled for so long was pouring into this one carnal act.

She felt her pussy clamping down as an orgasm hit her unexpectedly, and she choked on a loud cry as her body shook and spasmed. Desh gave a strangled exclamation as she squeezed around him, but he didn't stop fucking her. He pushed into her even harder, his grunts so loud they were almost shouts.

Then he was coming too, his face contorting and his body jerking clumsily as it rode out the spasms.

He'd obviously come hard, so hard it took everything he had. After his final bellow of release, he collapsed on top of her.

She held him with her arms and her legs, her body still making little aftershocks of pleasure as it relaxed.

They were both gasping loudly in the otherwise silent room, and Talia was so hot and damp that she thought she might melt.

Her body felt so incredibly good.

And so did her heart.

So did her heart.

She didn't want to let Desh go.

Eventually, however, her legs started to cramp up, so she carefully unwound them and stretched them out.

Desh moaned as his softened cock slipped out of her with a sound of wet suction. He finally lifted his weight off her as he rolled over onto his back, still panting unevenly.

She stroked his chest gently, and he turned his head to meet her eyes.

"It's okay for you to feel good sometimes," she murmured.

"I don't know." He shook his head slowly. "But there's no way I can help myself with you. You... shatter me."

She didn't know what to say to that.

He shattered her too.

Finally she said, "If you really think I'm not good for you, I don't have to come to your room anymore."

"You have to come," he said thickly. "I can't do without you anymore."

She smiled. She couldn't help it.

No one had ever felt that way about her before.

FIVE

Very late the following evening, Talia stretched out on Desh's bed, feeling relaxed and tired and a little sore.

Really good.

Really pleased with herself.

She was lying on her stomach, and she raised herself up on her arms enough to see over Desh's body to the console on the wall, which had beeped.

"You have a message," she said when she saw which light was blinking on the console.

Desh was lounging on his back, completely naked and with the covers pushed down to his waist. He gave her a lazy smile. "I'll check it later. It won't be important."

"How do you know?"

"I don't have anyone important who would be trying to contact me." He said the words with the easy nonchalance that spoke of living a long time on his own.

He wasn't a hard man. At all. She couldn't help but wonder why he was so completely alone.

Clearly unconcerned about the message, he reached over and trailed his fingertips down the line of her spine. She was as naked as he was. She'd even taken off her boots tonight. When he reached the small of her back, he lingered, brushing up and down the deep curve there. His eyes followed the motion of his hand.

"What is it?" she asked after a minute, starting to feel self-conscious at his lingering gaze, although his touch was light and pleasant.

"You are so beautiful," Desh murmured. "I love this spot right here."

She looked over her shoulder and tried to see the place on her body he was referring to. The dip just before the upward slope of her ass. "Uh, that's not normally the part of my body men most like to leer at."

"Then other men are crazy. It's absolutely delectable." He pulled the blanket down that had been covering her bottom, and his hand moved to cup one of the cheeks. "Of course, I love other parts of your body too."

Something about his expression was making her chest clench. It wasn't lust she saw in him right now. It wasn't desire as she understood it.

It was warm and soft and genuine. Real appreciation.

She wasn't used to it.

She wasn't sure how to respond to it.

Her cheeks flushed hotly, and she gave him a smile she hoped was seductive. His hand moved farther down and squeezed the back of her thighs, just under her butt.

"Now I know that's not the most attractive part of my body," she said, trying to break the tension in her chest with irony.

His eyes shot up to her face. "Why not?"

"Why not? Because there's a lot of extra fat there. I can't tell you how many times the others have told me never to take off my boots so my thighs can stay hidden."

"But that's ridiculous! Your thighs are incredibly sexy. All of you is gorgeous." His hand slid back up to caress her bottom, like he couldn't stop touching her.

He really seemed to mean what he said. "Well, thank you. But I've heard differently many times."

Desh frowned. "Why would they say things like that to you? Even if your thighs weren't perfect, there's nothing you could do about it. It just seems mean."

"It's not mean. The others are trying to help. Most of them anyway. I'm still really new at this, and it does help to get advice from others."

"So they... so they give you advice on how to have sex?"

"Of course. Why wouldn't they?"

"I don't know. It seems a little uncomfortable to me."

She chuckled and rolled over onto her side, pulling up the sheet to her waist. Desh's eyes moved immediately to her bare breasts, and he didn't seem to mind her repositioning. "It seems uncomfortable to you because you take sex personally. It's not personal to us. It's our job. So of course we need some help in how to do it better."

He was frowning again. "What kind of help do they give you?"

"Mostly just advice on how to handle certain kinds of partners and how men behave and what moves work best on them."

Desh cleared his throat. "So did you... you use their advice on me?"

She couldn't read his expression very well, so she didn't know what he wanted to hear. Not knowing anything else to say, she told him the truth. "Not really. Well, some obvious stuff they told me at the beginning, about how to do a good blow job. But I've never really gotten any advice about sex when... when I enjoy it."

A little smile was starting to play around the corners of his mouth. "Is that right?"

"Yes, that's right. I've never enjoyed it before. Does that make you feel special?"

He leaned over to brush her lips lightly with his. "Yes," he murmured. "It does."

She couldn't help but smile against his mouth.

"So what was it like?" Desh asked in a different tone, pulling back and reclining again. "When you started working here? Was it hard for you?"

She thought about the question for a minute before she answered. No one had ever asked her anything like it before. "I... I guess it was. I had no idea what I was doing. I was completely clueless."

"Clueless about sex?"

"Yes. Well, I knew what it was. We lived in a very small cottage in my home village, without very much privacy. I knew what sex was. But it was always something done in quiet in the dark, and I'd never done it myself."

"You were a virgin when you came here?" His voice was different, strangely breathless.

It made Talia feel... uncomfortable.

"Yes, I was a virgin. That's part of why I was chosen. Some men prefer virgins."

"So they just sent you off with some old perv when you'd never even had sex before?"

"It wasn't like that. He wasn't a mean man. It was... Well, it didn't feel good. It kind of hurt, but they'd told me to expect that. It wasn't traumatic or anything, so you don't need to look so horrified. They're careful about who they let the new girls pair up with. They don't want us to get hurt. I was fine with it. I did the best I could, and he seemed pleased with it, so I figured it was a success. Don't make me feel like I... I should feel bad about it."

She was talking too much, and her voice was breaking a little. She didn't know why his expression was making her feel this way.

"I don't want you to feel bad, Talia. I really don't. I just don't like the idea of your being hurt."

"I wasn't hurt. I'm telling you I wasn't. I wanted this job. I wanted to do it. You know, I used to stay awake at night when I was a girl and imagine a different life—one where I could have a room of my own and pretty clothes and grapes to eat."

"Grapes?"

"Yes, real grapes. Not replicated stuff. An old man I knew from my village would let me look at his books. Once, he'd managed to get his hands on some real grapes, and he gave me eight of them. I'd never tasted anything like them. I dreamed of them afterward. When I was seventeen, I had a choice about how I would spend my life. I could stay on that world and be a wife to someone I didn't like and never have... anything. Or I could come here—and have the chance at things I never could have gotten otherwise. Do you think I'm wrong for choosing this?"

"No! Not at all! Of course you made the right decision."

His obvious sincerity made her feel better. "It was the right decision. I knew it then. It felt weird to have sex that first time. It was hot and uncomfortable and kind of embarrassing. But I still knew it was better than what I had left behind. I was fine with it that first time. And I was happy that the man had chosen me."

"All right," he murmured. He'd reached out again, and his fingers were trailing down her arm the way they had her back earlier. "All right."

"It wasn't bad." She didn't know why she was still talking about it since he'd accepted what she'd said. "It wasn't. It's just sex. Nothing but sex. It's not like the first time would ever be special."

Desh's eyes rested on her face for a silent moment. Then he said very softly, "Mine was."

Her heart and her stomach both twisted with emotion, and there was nothing she could do to calm them down.

She had to get the attention off her before she did something really stupid like burst into tears. So she smiled and said, "So tell me about you."

He arched his eyebrows just slightly. "Uh, Talia, you know that you were with me for my first time, right?"

She giggled. "I didn't mean tell me about your first time. I meant tell me about your work. What was it like for you the first time you fought?"

He opened his mouth, enlightenment washing over his face as he understood her question. "Ah. Well, the first real fight I got into was on that undeveloped planet I told you about. I was sixteen, and I was attacked by these... cavemen. Needless to say, I wouldn't have survived if I hadn't been rescued."

"By who?"

"By other cavemen. Nicer ones." He shook his head. "I was so weak. So helpless."

"You were only sixteen."

"Still, a sixteen-year-old should have been able to do better than I did." He wasn't meeting her eyes, and she could see that the memory still rankled.

"So what did you do?"

"I let other people take care of me since I was helpless to take care of myself. I eventually learned a few things. I got a little better. I even killed an animal with a spear."

"Did you?" she asked, her eyes very wide. "Why?"

"To eat. Of course, it took three years to get to that point."

"I can't believe you were on that planet for so long. How did you get there to begin with?"

He cleared his throat. "I... I, uh, crashed there."

"And no one came to rescue you?"

"There wasn't anyone who would have wanted to rescue me."

The words were matter-of-fact, not self-pitying, but they sounded so incredibly lonely. She reached out to put a hand on his chest. "What about your family?"

"I don't have a family." Something new had entered his eyes, an expression she'd never seen there before.

It was hard—harder than the Desh she'd known. It scared her a little.

"Oh." She didn't know what to say.

After a long pause, Desh finally continued, "I only ever had a father. He was..."

She wanted to prompt him to continue, but he felt so tense she didn't dare. She just waited to see if he would go on.

He did. "He never wanted me. I was a status symbol mostly—a son who was so smart, who did so well in school. I loved him because he was my father, but he never loved me. He proved that very clearly."

Her heart was aching for the pain she could hear in his voice. She'd never bonded very closely with her own family either, but she'd also never felt betrayed by them in the way she could hear in Desh's voice. "What did he do?"

"He... he proved that his personal power was more important to him than I was. I was a fool to ever think it might be different." He shook his head slightly, as if scattering his bitter thoughts. "Anyway, he didn't come looking for me when I crashed on that planet. He... wanted to get rid of me when it was clear I couldn't improve his status. So I was stuck on that planet for years."

"Were those years miserable then?" she asked.

He shook his head. "Not really. They were hard. And lonely. The last year someone else... someone else crashed there too, and I liked her. So I had someone to talk to at last."

"She was your partner?" Talia asked, feeling a flicker of something that was unmistakably jealousy.

She didn't like the idea of Desh having a partner on the planet.

She didn't like it at all.

"No!" He gave an ironic laugh. "Not at all. She found herself a better, stronger man than me. But I liked her. We were friends."

That tension in her chest relaxed, although she didn't like how bitterly Desh remembered himself as weak.

"So it wasn't all terrible there then?"

"No. It wasn't terrible. It was... hard, but that doesn't always mean bad. There was something untouched about that planet, like I was living in a different time, like the Coalition world I knew could never touch it." His voice broke on the last couple of words, and he covered it with a cough.

Talia sat up. "Desh, what happened?"

He shook his head. He wouldn't meet her eyes. His shoulders were visibly tense.

"Desh, what about your friend? Is she all right?"

"Yes. She's all right. After we escaped, she went back because she loved her man there and life with him was better than what she had anywhere else. She thought it would be... She thought it would last. That world was innocent. Not the people there—they were like everyone else, some good and some bad—but the planet... the *planet* was innocent. And a lot was beautiful about it. It should have... lasted longer."

"Tell me what happened," Talia said hoarsely. She didn't know why she was so upset by this conversation, but she was. She could sense how deep it went with Desh, and so it felt deep to her too. "Didn't it last?"

"In Coalition space? You really think something beautiful and innocent could endure for long?"

"Oh no!"

He was still shaking his head, still staring at a space in the air. "She had nine years there before they came. The Coalition. To develop the planet. They called it *development*. What they did was razed everything good about it to the ground."

Talia was actually tearing up, although she didn't know why. "Is she okay?"

"Yes. She got out with her family. They went... they went somewhere else. Somewhere the Coalition hasn't yet reached. Some of the others got out too, but... their world was still destroyed."

Talia could barely speak over the lump in her throat. "That is why you left Mel Tana at last?" She didn't know how she knew this, but she did. "The bad news that wouldn't let you... sit still?"

Desh nodded mutely.

"You went to make sure she was all right?"

"Yes. Her and her family. And then..." He cleared his throat. "Sometimes things happen that are so wrong—so utterly wrong—that you can't just hide away any longer."

Her hand clenched on his chest. "So what are you going to do?" she whispered.

He seemed to realize what he'd said, and he shook off the intensity of the moment before. He smiled at her. "Right now I'm going to win the Tournament. I'll worry about the rest of it later."

She had more questions—a lot more she needed to know—but it was clear that was all the confessionals Desh was giving tonight.

The following night, she went back to his room, and after she walked through the door, before she'd had a chance to say anything, her attention was distracted by a bowl on the table, sitting next to the medical device she'd kept from the med unit so she could treat any further of Desh's injuries.

It was a large silver bowl.

Filled with lovely purple grapes.

She gasped as she processed them, her hand coming up to cover her mouth.

Desh looked a little sheepish as he stood beside her.

When she was able to move, she turned to stare at him in wonder.

He gave a half shrug. "You said yesterday you... They're pretty hard to get, even here, but I've earned enough so far in the Tournament that I could afford them. I thought you might... like them."

"You got them for me?"

"Well, yes. Who else?"

Her eyes had filled with tears, blurring her vision. She was shaking with emotion. She couldn't say anything.

"I had one. They're really good. You said you... you used to dream about them. So I thought..." He gave another of those half shrugs, his eyes searching her face as if trying to figure out how she was feeling.

She gave a little sob and walked over to the table. She reached out to pluck one of the grapes from the bunch and stared at it in her hand.

"Go ahead," Desh said, stepping over beside her. "Try it."

She popped the grape into her mouth. As soon as she bit down, an explosion of crisp sweetness overwhelmed her taste buds, filled her senses.

It was exactly as she remembered from when she'd first tasted them at six years old.

A tear streamed down her face, and she brushed it away impatiently.

She turned to smile up at Desh, feeling like something had burst into light inside her. "Thank you," she managed to say after she'd swallowed.

His expression softened. "You're welcome." He gestured toward the table. "You can have more than one, you know. We can maybe save some for tomorrow, but they don't last very long without getting squishy."

"You know a lot about grapes."

"Not really. Although I did meet a couple once who owned a vineyard."

"Really?"

"Yes. They taught me a little about grapes. They grew them to make wine. Have some more."

She couldn't resist, and together they ate about half the bowl. Talia enjoyed them so much she was almost limp afterward, and Desh was starting to get a little grumpy about the number of times she was thanking him.

"You don't have to thank me again," he grumbled after about her fifth attempt to express her gratitude. "It wasn't that big a deal."

"It was to me," she said. "No one has ever done something so nice for me before."

He looked at her for a long time. Then he finally shook his head. "Someone should have done nice things for you a long time ago."

"Can I do something nice for you now?"

His forehead wrinkled. "Do what?"

She stood up and untied her tunic, letting it slip from her shoulders onto the floor.

Desh's eyes raked over her body, and his cheeks flushed as his posture tightened. He always responded to her that way. He really liked how she looked.

He was still sitting in a straight chair by the table, and she stepped closer to him. "You don't have to..." He cleared his throat. "You don't have to do anything. I didn't give you grapes because I expected..."

"I know you didn't. But I want to do something nice for you now."

He stared at her hotly as she leaned over to run her hands down his chest and abdomen.

Then she added, "I would have done it for you anyway, even without the grapes." Her hands ended up on his cock, which had grown hard in his trousers.

He let out a soft moan as she squeezed him, and his hips bucked up eagerly into her grip. "If you... if you..."

"I like to please you," she murmured hoarsely, lowering herself onto her knees on the floor. "I like that you seem to enjoy it."

"Enjoy it?" he rasped, bucking up again as she reached into his trousers to get her hands around his erection. "Enjoy it? You... you intoxicate me."

That sounded pretty good. She smiled as she lowered her mouth to his cock.

He cupped her head with both hands as she started to work him over, and soon he was groaning helplessly and rocking his pelvis up into her sucking.

He still didn't have much control. He was always urgent and excited with her, not able to hold himself back for very long, and tonight he was more so than usual.

As she hollowed out her cheeks, he moved against her clumsily, tightening his hands and thighs as his groaning turned to breathless grunts.

He wasn't forceful like so many men she knew—who tried to fuck her throat because they could. Desh always tried to be careful, even when he was on the verge of losing it.

Soon his whole body was tensing up and his cock was shuddering in her mouth. Then he choked on a loud roar as he let go, and she sucked him through a long series of spasms.

He fell back into the chair when she finally let his cock slip from her lips, and he was smiling tiredly when she moved her eyes to his face.

"It looks like you enjoyed that," she said, straightening her back and rubbing his thighs soothingly. His whole body was starting to relax now.

"Enjoy doesn't even come close." He reached down for her and pulled her into his lap, cradling her against him.

She snuggled against him, loving the feel of his arms as much as the rest of his body.

She'd never been held like this before.

It made her feel... special, precious.

He was quiet for a long time as he recovered from his climax and just held her. Then he finally murmured into the silence, "If you could be anywhere in the universe, where would you be? What would you do?"

She blinked and raised her head from where she'd been resting it against his shoulder. "I... I don't know."

"You don't have daydreams?"

"Of course I do. But I usually dream about the books I read. All those old stories of courage and adventure and heroes saving their people. About uprisings, throwing off oppression. Sometimes..." She paused, lowering her voice as she continued, "Sometimes I imagine how it would happen here."

He tightened his arms around her. "You really daydream about that?"

"Yes. I do. I like to... I know it sounds ridiculous, but I make all these plans and plots. There are little rebellions all over, so I plan out ways to somehow bring them all together..." She giggled. "I know, it's crazy, but you asked. It... it makes me feel better."

He stroked her hair as she cuddled against him again. "You don't daydream about being happy?"

"I think... that *is* me dreaming of being happy. I don't know how else I ever could be. I guess I do sometimes daydream about having a room of my own, having privacy, being able to get real fruit occasionally. That's as happy as I can imagine being in this world. In this world as it is now."

"It doesn't sound like much."

"It's better than I had before." She listened to him breathe for a minute. Then she asked, "What about you? What do you daydream about? If you could be anywhere in the universe where would you be?"

He let out a sigh. "That planet with the vineyard I mentioned. That's the same one where my friend and her family ended up going. If I have... if I have any friends in the universe, they're on that planet."

"So why don't you live there too?"

He shook his head. "I don't think I could be happy with so much... so much wrong. It would always feel like it was lurking on the outskirts of my mind. And the truth is I don't know how long that planet can remain a safe haven. How long will it be before they come and destroy that world too?"

"So you don't know of anywhere you could be happy?"

"I don't think I'm... called to be happy."

She sucked in a breath and straightened up again. "What does that mean? What are you called to do, if not to be happy?"

"What are any of us called to do? Do the best we can with what we have." He leaned forward to kiss her gently. "I have this time with you at least. I never believed I could feel this way."

"What way?"

"Good. I feel good."

She stared at him for a long time before she was able to admit, "I didn't believe I could ever feel this good either."

~

Eight days later, after another round of the Tournament, she showed up at Desh's door.

She'd been to his room almost every night for the past two weeks. If she had another appointment in the evening, she went to his room afterward.

Jenelle said it was too much. She said it was dangerous to spend that much time with a man who couldn't afford to pay for exclusivity. But Talia didn't care.

The Tournament would be over next week, and then Desh would be leaving the Residence.

She wanted to spend as much time as she could with him before he did.

His doors slid open, and she stepped into his room, and he was on her before she knew what was happening. He pushed her against the wall, kissing her deep and hard.

She responded immediately, her heart leaping in excitement.

She'd never in her life known that kissing could feel so good, like he was so deep inside her she'd never be alone again.

They kissed until they were rocking together, and then he took her right there against the wall, lifting her hips and holding her steady as he fucked her with fast, short thrusts.

Then he carried her over to the bed and moved on top of her, holding on to her bottom as he took her with primal urgency. She came and came again and was biting her lip to keep from screaming as he finally fell out of rhythm.

Both of them were urgent and sweating and grunting loudly as they worked up to a final peak. Talia felt her body fly apart again as Desh finally fell over the edge too.

It took them a long time to catch their breaths and come to their senses afterward, but both of them were smiling when they did.

"I guess you had a lot of pent-up energy tonight," she said. His head was against her shoulder, and she stroked his hair gently. "It really wasn't much of a fight."

Desh had won earlier this evening without getting too badly injured. It hadn't been an easy fight, but he'd kept in control the whole time. He would advance now to the final round next week.

"I think you had some pent-up energy too," he murmured, pressing a kiss into her skin.

She giggled. "Maybe a little. I got all excited when you won earlier."

He tilted his head to smile up at her, and her heart did a little melting thing that she knew wasn't smart.

He was only here temporarily.

She couldn't let herself bond with him.

He could never make her his favorite even if he wanted to.

Even with the winnings from the Tournament, he wouldn't be able to afford it for long.

She didn't like to think about his leaving after the Tournament was over, so she intentionally pushed it from her mind.

If she thought about it, she wouldn't enjoy the time she had.

They lay together in comfortable silence until she asked idly, "What were you like as a boy?"

He blinked, obviously surprised by the question. "I don't know. Not very interesting."

"Why do you say that?"

"All I did was study. I told you I was pretty much a nerd."

"Was your family academic?"

"N-not really. But I guess I showed early signs of being good at school, so I was in an accelerated curriculum by the time I was seven. I had more than one advanced degree by the time I was sixteen."

"That was when you crashed on that planet?"

"Yeah."

"Where were you going... that would have crashed like that? And why didn't your parents search for you?"

He didn't answer.

The silence stretched so long that she lifted her head to study his face. "Desh?"

He sighed. "It was a planet dump."

Her whole body jerked. "What? A planet dump? As a... a punishment?"

"Yes. That's why no one searched for me. Because I was supposed to be gone."

She was breathing fast and hard, trying to keep up with this piece of information. "What had you done?"

He shook his head. "Not much. Said something to the wrong person. They called it... sedition."

"Sedition? What did you say?"

"You know all the stories you read—about revolts and uprisings. They're all based on a few main ideals. What I said was something akin to those ideals. But I said it to the wrong person. He... he didn't take it well."

She thought about that for a minute, and she decided none of it was surprising. Not in Coalition space. Even with the trappings of advanced civilization, people were still treated barbarically. Capital punishment might be banned, but criminals were treated just as poorly—sent to prison planets for the rest of their lives or dropped on hostile planets to fend for themselves or die.

And the crimes that warranted those punishments could be nothing at all.

That was how the Coalition had kept control of so many worlds for so long. Even the smallest of crimes were life sentences.

"I'm sorry," she said at last. "That shouldn't have happened to you."

"I knew better," he murmured thickly. "I knew better. I thought... maybe I hoped I would be treated differently, but I wasn't. Maybe I'm better off this way."

"All alone and on some doomed mission?" She still didn't know what he was trying to accomplish here, but she was convinced it wasn't good.

"Yes. At least there are no illusions."

Someone had hurt him in the past. A lot. Someone had betrayed his trust.

He'd believed someone would protect him who hadn't done so.

She could only assume it was a member of his family.

She hated the person—intensely—even though she had no idea who it was.

She hated anyone who would hurt someone as gentle as Desh.

"If they sentenced you as a criminal, how did you get through security to come to the Residence?" she asked after reflecting for a minute.

"It's not hard to get identity records changed. I had someone create a new identity for me before I even went to Mel Tana—fingerprints, DNA, all of it."

"And no one would recognize you?"

He let out a little breath. "No one that I've seen yet."

She lifted her head. "That doesn't sound good. I guess that's why you're always wearing that mask out in public. But still, if you're recognized, you'll be in big trouble."

"I know. But by the time someone recognizes me, it will be too late."

She didn't know what that meant, but it sounded bleak. "But—"

"I've got everything worked out, Talia. I'm not going to be recognized."

She pressed her lips together and held back another objection. He clearly didn't want to talk about it with her.

If she kept it up, he would get annoyed with her. Then he might even kick her out or decide to stop seeing her.

She was supposed to be a professional, although she wasn't acting like it lately.

She reached out to stroke his hair and changed the subject. "Why didn't you go back to school afterward? After you were rescued, I mean. You don't care about learning anymore?"

He gave a little shrug. "It all felt... useless."

That made her sad.

Really sad.

That something he'd loved before felt useless to him now.

He was damaged in so many ways, and there was nothing she could do to answer it.

"You still read though? You were in the library that day reading, weren't you?"

"Yes." He made a face that clearly expressed his distaste for seeing her fuck the subcommander that day a few weeks ago.

"So it seems like you might still have some interest in learning."

"Maybe. But it's just a hobby now. It's too late for anything else."

"Why?"

He looked at her, naked feeling in his eyes, but he didn't answer her question.

After a minute, he brushed a kiss into her hair. "You love to read. Maybe you should go study."

She gave a huff of ironic amusement. "It's too late for me too."

All she had left were her daydreams, and those dreams never got to the end.

The end of the dreams of revolt she had would never be good.

As she lay beside him in his bed, she tried to imagine what it might be like if Desh would somehow be able to make her his favorite, if she wouldn't have to fuck anyone else but Desh.

Ever.

It was such a tantalizing and lovely fantasy that she let it play in her mind for a while until she realized what she was doing.

Jenelle was right.

Romanticizing was dangerous.

She could let herself hope for something she knew would never happen, and it would only crush her in the end.

Desh was either going to win the Tournament or he would be defeated next week. Either way, he would leave.

He wasn't a Coalition high official. He could never make her his favorite.

And dreaming about it wasn't good for her.

He would move on, and she would remain here, pleasing other men.

Even if Desh was the only man she wanted.

SIX

A few days later, Talia felt slightly nauseated as she rose to her feet in front of Marshall.

She'd been with him a few times a week for the past few weeks. Not every day. Not nearly as often as she'd been with Desh. But he'd made several very generous donations to the leisure suite, and it would be stupid and unprofessional for her to stop seeing him.

He'd found her this afternoon, and she'd given him a blow job. She knew what got to him now, and she'd made sure he'd come quickly because she really didn't feel like having him fuck her today.

She shouldn't be feeling that way.

It was bad.

It was dangerous.

It would only make it harder once Desh left the Residence.

She should never have let herself fall for Desh so much that she didn't even want to do her job.

Marshall seemed pleased and sated as she got to her feet, so at least she hadn't messed things up with him. He was a much more promising possibility for her future than Desh would ever be. He'd be stationed in or near the Residence for at least a year and maybe longer.

She needed to keep remembering that.

"That was something else," he said with a flushed face and a particularly satisfied smile. "You know how to use that little mouth."

She smiled and dropped her lashes and tried to calm the roiling of her stomach.

This wasn't right.

This wasn't the way she should be feeling.

She shouldn't want to gag just because she had another man's cock in her mouth.

She could be good at this, but only if she kept her heart out of business. That was the first rule of working as a leisure escort, and it was the one that really mattered.

"I dropped by the suite the other night to look for you, but they said you were busy."

Her spine stiffened at this comment, but she managed to hold on to her shy expression. "I'm sorry I missed you."

"I guess you were with someone else?"

It was more than likely Desh she'd been with since she'd gone to his room every night for weeks. She made a wordless hum as a response.

"How many other men are you seeing?" Marshall asked.

She gasped and raised her eyes to his face. "What do you mean?"

"How many other men are you seeing right now?"

She swallowed. "It depends. Some just drop by occasionally."

"How much would it take to get you to stop seeing them?"

Her eyes widened dramatically, and her heart dropped dramatically. "There's…. there's not a set amount. But it's a lot."

He nodded, looking thoughtful. "I'm not saying I'll do it, but I might check it out. I like the idea of always having you at my disposal, and I don't like having to wait for you to finish up with someone else."

This was a dream come true.

It was better than her wildest expectations.

She was only eighteen years old, and she might become the favorite of a man of significant status.

She'd assumed it would be years before she got to that point.

Only her fantasies had changed over the past month.

Now what she wanted was something else.

And despite her attempt to be excited about his words, she felt sicker than ever.

If he donated enough money to the suite to make her his favorite, then she wouldn't be able to see Desh.

Ever again.

She'd made it back to the leisure suite and was about to enter through the main doors when they slid open and Desh stepped out.

She gasped loudly at his sudden appearance.

He was wearing the mask as he always did outside his room, but she would recognize his body anywhere.

She stopped in her tracks when he turned his head and saw her.

"Hi," she said with a little smile. "Were you... were you looking for me?"

"Of course." He frowned and came over to stand just in front of her. "You didn't think I'd want to see someone else, did you?"

She hadn't.

She couldn't imagine Desh wanting to see another escort.

And just the thought of his doing so made her want to dig her fingernails into her palms.

Another sign that her feelings were all in chaos where he was concerned.

"I wasn't..." She cleared her throat. "I wasn't expecting you."

"I know. I was just..." He didn't finish the sentence. Instead, he asked, "Are you free right now?"

"Yes. I am. Did you want to do something?" She wondered if he'd gotten horny this afternoon and hadn't wanted to wait until tonight. Why else would he be here?

"It's a nice day. Maybe we could take a walk or something?"

All right. Evidently he hadn't just been wanting to fuck her. "Of course. We can go to the guest gardens."

She felt strangely nervous and uncertain as she walked beside him through the corridors until they'd reached the doors that led out to the expansive gardens cultivated for guests' enjoyment. There were also private gardens in the Residence for the High Director, as well as a dedicated garden for the leisure suite.

Like all gardens in and around Earth, the climate was carefully adjusted to ensure plants were blooming all year round.

Desh was strangely quiet as they started walking along one of the trails, surrounded by an explosion of colorful tropical flowering plants.

"Are you all right?" she asked after a few minutes, starting to worry about his silence.

"Yes."

She didn't know what to say to that so she didn't say anything.

"Were you... were you with someone else just now?" Desh asked after a minute. His eyes were focused straight ahead, and she couldn't see his expression behind his mask.

"Y-yes."

He inhaled and then let out the breath.

She closed her hands into fists at her sides, her stomach twisting even more than it had earlier with Marshall. "You know I see other men."

"Yes. I know." His voice was thicker than it should have been.

"You're not... you're not angry about that, are you?"

"No. I'm not angry."

"This is my job."

"I know it is."

"Desh." She stopped walking and turned to face him, reaching up to take off the mask since it was frustrating her to not be able to see his face.

He backed away, preventing her from taking the mask off.

She was so upset by his reaction that she let out a little whimper. "You're really mad at me?"

"No. I said I wasn't mad."

"But you're acting—"

"We can't talk about this here." He glanced around as if checking to see if anyone else was around.

Understanding he wanted privacy, she took his hand and led him into a small gazebo and pressed the button to pull the automated shades down, closing them off from the rest of the garden.

Desh took his mask off then, and she saw that he wasn't angry after all.

He looked upset. Not angry.

"Desh," she said, her throat closing up around her emotion. "Desh, you can't act this way."

His jaw clenched. "I'm trying not to."

"Well, you need to try harder because this isn't fair to me. This is my job."

"I know it's your job. I don't have to like it, do I?"

"It's been my job since the first day we met. You knew it was my job all along. If you had a problem with it, you shouldn't have done anything with me."

"I know that. I *know* that." He was breathing quickly, and he'd turned his face away, as if he were trying to get himself under control.

"Why is this suddenly bothering you?"

He swallowed visibly and turned to meet her eyes again. "Because I never let myself think about it before. I just pretended... I didn't let myself think about it. But then I came to see you right now, and you weren't in, and they implied you were with someone else. And one of the women in there, she gave me this smile... like she was teasing me with what you were doing with some other man..." He sucked in a ragged breath and turned his head away again.

Talia knew—she *knew*—that the woman who had teased him was Breann. Breann had always been that way.

She reached out and turned Desh's head so he was facing her again. "I'm sorry it bothered you, but there's nothing I can do about it. This is my job, and if I don't do it, then I'll lose any chance of a comfortable future."

He took both her hands in his and gave her a deep, searching look. "And this is the future you want? Fucking any man who wants you?"

She jerked her hands out his grip, feeling like she'd just been slapped. She turned and took a few steps away, fighting a sudden flood of tears.

"I'm sorry," Desh murmured roughly, coming over and putting his hands on her shoulders so she was facing him again. "I'm sorry. That was a horrible thing to say." He took another one of those ragged breaths before he continued, "I know this is your job, and I know there's nothing shameful about it. But I've never been able to... I know I'm supposed to be cool and sophisticated and live in this world where sex is just something you do for fun, but I'm not. And I don't. Sex is still personal to me. And it feels personal with you. It feels... really personal." His voice trailed off until the last words were almost mumbled.

Talia was confused and excited and trembling, and she didn't even know why. She twisted her hands together and stared at him.

Desh lifted his eyes to meet hers again. "So it really doesn't feel personal to you? Being with me?"

She swayed on her feet. She covered her mouth with one hand and searched for an answer to a question that had utterly leveled her. "I... I don't know."

"You really don't know?"

Her legs wouldn't support her for much longer, so she stepped backward until she could sit on a cushioned bench. "It does feel different with you," she admitted. "I like being with you in a way I've never liked being with anyone else."

He took two long strides over so he could sit beside her. "So I'm not wrong that what we have is... personal?"

"I don't know. It shouldn't be personal. I shouldn't let it get personal." She stared down at the pale gray floor. "If I have, then I've really messed up."

He cupped her cheek with one big hand. "You haven't messed up, Talia."

She pulled her head away from his palm. "Yes, I have. Because this is my job, and that's not going to change. And if you get upset that I'm with other men, then I'm going to have to… have to stop seeing you. I have to think about what's best for me."

She knew what was best for her.

There was only one answer.

Marshall had said he was thinking of making her his favorite.

By any reasonable standard, that would be the best option. It would make her safest, more secure, most comfortable.

Desh winced slightly, as if she'd leveled him a blow. He lowered his hand to his lap and said slowly, "I want what's best for you too."

He meant it.

He really meant it.

"This is my life, Desh," she said softly. "And it's not a bad one. Right now, if I hadn't come to work in the leisure suite, I would be married to a gross old man back on my home planet. I've told you that before. I didn't know enough back then to recognize it, but he would have treated me terribly. I can see that now. I'd be married to that man, or I'd still be living with my family and trying to scrape by enough to live on. Those would have been my only two options for a future. You understand, we didn't have enough money to even try starting a life somewhere else. So do you really think I made the wrong decision in coming here?"

"No! Of course you didn't. I never meant to imply otherwise. You did the best you could with the options available. You've done... amazingly well for yourself. You're... amazing."

She swallowed hard, still feeling like she might cry at any moment. "So this is the best thing for me—to do the best I can in the life I have here. It has to be the best thing for me. There's not... another option. Is there?"

She didn't know why she asked the last wistful question. It was foolish and weak, and she knew better than to even hope.

There wasn't another option.

Not for her life.

Not for most people's lives.

Not living in a universe like this one.

"No," Desh said hoarsely. He wasn't looking at her now. "I wish I could... I can't give you another option."

She'd known that from the beginning.

Jenelle had told her from the first day she'd arrived. Romanticizing only led to heartache.

It hurt anyway, hearing that answer from Desh.

Talia had to breathe for a minute or two until she got herself under control again.

"All right," she said at last, pleased that her voice sounded mostly natural. "So I have to do my job and build the best future I can for myself here. No one else is going to take care of me. I have to take care of myself. I can keep seeing you as long as you're here, if you're all right with me also seeing other men. If you're not all right with it, then I can't see you anymore. What do you... what do you want?"

Desh stared at her for a long time. Then he finally murmured, "I can't stop seeing you, Talia. Not yet. I know we don't have very much time, but I can't give you up yet."

Her hands were shaking again. "And you're all right with me seeing other men?"

"Not really. Not... really. But I'll make myself be."

It wasn't much of an answer, but she could see he was genuinely trying. She nodded, telling herself that things were settled so she could act like herself again.

She was still trying to convince herself of this when Desh kissed her.

Her attempts to think reasonably evaporated into nothing as she experienced a deep wave of longing. Her hands flew up to tangle in his hair, and she leaned into his lips, slipping her tongue out to meet his eagerly.

He sucked in a breath through his nose, holding her head with one hand and sliding the other one down her back. He eased her down until she was lying on the bench and he was pressed on top of her.

His warm body rubbed against hers, and his tongue slid even deeper into her mouth, teasing it in a way that made her entire body clench in pleasure.

It was a long time before he finally tore his mouth away and stared down at her in hot stupor.

"What?" she whispered, raising her hips to grind herself against his erection because her pussy was aching with arousal.

He groaned and winced slightly at her move, but his gaze remained fixed on her face.

"What?" she demanded again, aware of a new feeling twisting in her belly.

Not just lust.

Something else.

Something deeper.

Something absolutely terrifying.

"I want you to want me," Desh murmured at last.

Her lips parted. "Of course I want you. Why do you think I'm rubbing against you this way?"

He shook his head. "I want you to want me for real. All the way. Not just your body."

She panted, unable to look away from his blue eyes. She had no idea what to say.

She did want him.

More than her body wanted him.

But it was dangerous—so dangerous—in so many ways.

"I love your body," Desh said with that same rasp in his throat. He reached down to untie her tunic and pull the fabric apart, baring her completely. He cupped one of her breasts gently, and she arched up into his palm. "But your body isn't the only thing I want."

"What..." She had to pause to gasp as he rubbed the heel of his hand over her nipple. "What else do you want?"

"I want all of you." He moved his other hand so he was holding both her breasts. "And I want all of you to want me."

She rolled her hips restlessly as desire clenched tightly between her legs.

Her heart was clenching too, making her throat ache, her eyes ache.

"This is all of me," she said at last, her voice weak and uncertain.

He shook his head. "No, it's not. I know it's not. You're holding back on me."

"But I..." She whimpered as he slid his hands up to cup her cheeks.

"You think I'm like all the rest of them, that all I want is your body."

"What else is... is there?" She was almost writhing now. Her body wanted him badly, but something stronger was coiling in her heart—something so new and so dangerous and so uncertain that she couldn't allow it to exist.

No matter how much she wanted it.

No matter how much she wanted to give it to this man leaning above her, something she'd never seen before on his face.

"There's you. The whole you. I want to make love to all of it, not just your body."

Her eyes were blurring over, and she couldn't hold her hips still. No one said make love anymore. It was an archaic expression. People had sex, they fucked, they took what they wanted.

They took what they wanted from her.

"I'm... I'm just me. There's nothing else I can give you," she said at last when she could finally make her voice work.

He leaned down even farther to brush his lips against hers. So softly.

Too softly.

A couple of tears slid out of her eyes.

He murmured against her lips. "Then I'll give all of me to you."

She shook beneath him as he deepened the kiss, and she kept shaking as he kissed his way down her face and her neck. He trailed his mouth along her pulse line and then her collar bones, pausing to suck, to tease, to nibble until she was moaning helplessly.

When he reached her breasts, he took one nipple between his lips, and she started to dig her fingernails into his shoulders. The stimulation was erotic torture, but it didn't come close to equaling the need she could feel in her heart.

She needed him to answer it.

She needed him to fill it.

She didn't even understand the emptiness, but she knew he was strong enough, gentle enough, to meet it.

He kissed his way all the way down her shuddering belly until he was nuzzling between her legs. She gave a little sob as he parted her with his fingers and then darted his tongue out to her entrance.

She fisted her hands in his hair as he explored with his tongue, and she cried out loudly when he found her clit. "Right there," she gasped, trying futilely to hold her hips still. "Oh, right there. Please."

He focused his attention on that spot, flicking it with his tongue and then closing his lips down to suck at her clit, and it was only a minute until she lost control completely, coming hard against his mouth. She thrashed as the sensations overwhelmed her, and she held his head in place until the spasms had all worked through her.

She was still moaning shamelessly between her panting as he moved back up her body. His eyes were still deep and possessive. They saw her. They knew her.

In a way no one ever had.

He kissed her mouth, and she could taste herself on him, but she didn't even care. He slid two fingers inside her pussy as he kissed her, and she pumped her hips automatically against the penetration.

He kept kissing her as he fucked her with his fingers, and then his thumb pressed down on her clit.

She climaxed again, groaning into his mouth and clawing lines down his back.

"I can feel you coming around my fingers," he murmured, finally breaking the kiss. "You're so hot and wet and sweet and tight. I never knew anything could feel so good. I just never knew."

"But you're not even..." She was almost in tears, and she sniffed and licked her lips. She couldn't possibly finish a complete sentence. Her body was still rocking, trying to ride his fingers. She couldn't get enough. "Desh, Desh, oh please! I need... I need..."

He kept moving his fingers inside her and massaging her clit until she came again, and she knew he was watching her as she did.

Her body was limp and so hot it felt like her skin was burning. She hadn't had time to catch her breath when she reached for him, trying to pull him into position between her legs. "Now you, Desh," she gasped. "I want you. I want *you.*"

"You have me." He reached into his trousers to pull out his cock, and then he positioned it at her entrance. "This is me. You have all of me."

She stared up at him with wide eyes as he slowly eased himself inside her.

She cried out at the thick penetration and wrapped her legs around him, hooking her heels to keep them in place.

He gazed down at her. "This is all of me," he murmured. "I'm yours."

It was too much. Too good. Too deep.

She didn't know how to handle it.

It would have been easier if he'd been demanding, if he'd kept wanting to take something from her, but he wasn't, he didn't.

He was generous.

He wasn't trying to please himself.

He was trying to please her.

She whimpered and rocked her hips up into him, needing to move, to break the aching tension in her heart.

His features twisted as she rode him from below, and she saw the moment when his control snapped. He groaned low and lingering as he started to pump his hips.

Their motion was fast and urgent and raw, and she kept her legs wrapped around him tightly. Her hands had moved down to his ass, and she was clawing at the firm flesh the way she had his back earlier. Her pussy was fluttering again, and she bit her bottom lip as she felt the orgasm deepening.

"Talia," Desh rasped. "You're... you're... everything."

She came in a sudden rush, crying out loudly as she did. He kept thrusting into her clenching, and it felt so good for so long that she kept sobbing out her pleasure until he reached the peak himself.

He rode out his climax with clumsy eagerness, choking out her name and other words, other words that were so unfamiliar she couldn't process them.

Then he moaned as his body finally grew still, his eyes opening to meet hers one more time.

He collapsed on top of her, the release of tension wiping him out. He panted against her neck, still mumbling out things she couldn't let herself hear.

Her hands moved of their own accord, caressing his back, his head, his hair. Soothing over the scratches she'd made in her eagerness.

She liked how relaxed he felt now. How warm and soft and heavy. How sated. How needy, as if he wanted her still, even after he'd found his release.

After a few minutes, he was able to move, but he didn't pull off her. He just moved a hand down to stroke her thigh, which was still lifted as her legs were wrapped around him.

"Talia," he murmured at last, raising his head so he could gaze down at her. His hand was squeezing the flesh between her bottom and thigh possessively.

As if it were his.

As if she were his.

He'd told her he was hers.

"I've never been with another woman," he said.

She swallowed hard. "I know."

"I might not be as good at this as other men."

She shook her head urgently. "You are, Desh. You are. You're... better."

She wasn't trying to flatter him. She was telling the naked truth.

He seemed to understand that she meant it. "I wish I knew more so I could give you more, but this is all I have. This is... all I am."

She raised a hand to his face. She couldn't help it. Tears were slipping out of her eyes again. "You're the best man I've ever known."

His features twisted briefly, as if her words meant something to him. He leaned down to kiss her again gently, briefly. "I wish I could give you more, everything, but..."

Of course there was a but.

There was always a but.

He couldn't offer her another option for her life.

She'd known it before they'd had sex, and nothing had changed since then.

It felt like something had changed—like she had changed, like everything had changed—but she was still an escort in the High Director's Residence, and Desh couldn't take her away from that.

No one could.

Which meant wanting something different— something more—was the worst thing she could possibly do to herself.

She made a little whine in her throat as a wave of terror overwhelmed her. She wriggled beneath him until he heaved himself up to a sitting position.

She scrambled to sit up, tying her robe as she did.

"What's the matter, Talia?" he asked.

She shook her head, not meeting his eyes.

"What's the matter?" he asked in a different tone. He sounded almost scared. "Sweetheart?"

"Don't call me that!" she snapped, so scared she sounded harsher than she'd intended.

He blinked. "I'm sorry. Just tell me what's wrong."

She shook her head and stared at the floor. "It's not fair for you to want everything from me. It's not fair. Not when you can't give me everything."

He was silent for a long time as he processed her words. Then he said very slowly, softly, "You're right. It's not fair. But I do. I still do."

She shot him a quick look. "You're... you're going to leave when the Tournament is over. Aren't you?"

He opened his mouth as if he was going to object, but then he shut it again. He didn't answer.

"And I'm going to stay here and keep doing my job. It's not fair for you to demand something from me that you're not willing to give."

"You have everything from me," Desh said, reaching out for her before she pulled away from his grip. "Everything I'm able to give, you have."

There was a qualification in his words. She heard it. And she'd known it before he'd spoken them out loud.

He cared about her. That seemed real. And he might want things to be different.

But they weren't different.

She was an escort.

And she wasn't his priority. Something else was first in his heart.

She didn't know what it was, but she'd felt it from the very beginning.

He was running into something—racing toward it with all his might—and that something wasn't her.

Jenelle had been right all along.

Talia had been foolish. Young and so foolish.

She'd allowed herself to get hurt—with nothing in the world to show for it.

She contorted her face to keep from crying as she stood up.

"Don't leave, sweetheart," Desh said, standing up too. "At least let me—"

"Don't call me that!" She gave him an icy glare—one that didn't match the wailing in her heart—and then she took a deep breath. "I can't see you again."

"But—"

"No. That's it. This isn't good for me. This is over."

He was still arguing, still reaching for her, but she couldn't let him touch her. She backed away from him, giving him one last fleeting look before she turned around and ran.

She managed to make it to the suite and then slip into her sleeping pod without anyone stopping her.

Then she was finally alone, finally had privacy to cry.

It was worse—so much worse—to have a taste of something better, deeper, than what her life could offer.

It was better when she hadn't known what she was missing.

It was better when she'd believed she was really just a body and that being with someone else could never really touch her soul.

It was better when her only fantasies were fighting for a dream of freedom she hadn't really believed existed.

She knew differently now.

And it made everything worse.

~

She didn't go to the last round of the Tournament that night. She should have gone, but she pretended to be sick.

She couldn't stand to see Desh again, even from a distance.

121

He won though.

He won the entire Tournament.

She heard all about it afterward.

The fight had taken about twenty minutes, and it had been raw and vicious and bloody. Desh had been injured with bones broken and ribs cracked, but the other fighter had finally submitted.

Desh had stood by himself in the center ring of the arena as the crowds had roared with his victory.

He hadn't raised his hands. He hadn't smiled. He hadn't done anything but stand there and eventually limped out of the ring.

She lay in bed for hours that night, wanting desperately to go to him.

He was injured and would need to be taken care of. The med device was still in his room, but it might be hard to operate himself.

He might not even do it.

He might just sit there and suffer.

He'd told her he was here to answer what was wrong in the world, and that meant something more than winning the Tournament.

She racked her mind for what it might be, and every idea she came up with terrified her.

She wanted so much to go to him.

She knew better now however. She was stronger and wiser and more like Jenelle.

She wasn't going to buy into silly ideas of love and romance.

Desh might want her, but he didn't want her enough.

And she didn't live in a world where a truth like that could ever change.

SEVEN

The next day, Talia was sitting in the common room of the suite, trying to act like everything was normal.

It wasn't normal.

It was miserable.

And the days, weeks, months, years of her life that would follow this morning felt equally miserable, interminable.

But she didn't know what she could do about it.

Maybe it had always been this way, and she'd been too blind to know it.

When the main doors slid open, all the escorts in the room straightened up, hoping for a new partner who would choose them.

Talia didn't straighten up—not until she saw the newcomer was Desh. He was dressed in his normal clothes and wearing his Combatant's mask.

After remaining frozen for a moment, processing his presence and the surge of joy and then fear that followed it, she got up to walk out of the room.

"Talia," he said, striding over toward her. "Don't leave."

She stopped. Doing otherwise would cause a scene, and everyone's eyes were on her right now.

"I wanted to talk," Desh said in a softer voice.

She looked at him blankly, her throat not working enough to form a response.

It was wrong. It didn't make sense.

There was no reason for her heart to have exploded into feeling like this from nothing more than his standing so close to her.

His eyes searched her face, but as he opened his mouth to speak, he seemed suddenly aware that they were in the middle of a room full of other people, all of whom were watching them curiously.

"Can we talk somewhere?" he asked hoarsely.

"We can talk here."

"Somewhere private?"

"I told you yesterday—"

"I know what you told me. I just want to talk. Nothing else."

He seemed to mean it, and ridiculously his sincerity hurt her. Proof that whatever they'd had was over.

But it was clearly for the best, so she nodded stiffly and then gestured down the hall that led to the playrooms.

Most of them were empty at this time of day, so she made her way down the end of the hall to the very last one.

It was the smallest and the simplest, with no sexy paraphernalia or decorations.

Her body was already reacting to Desh's presence beside her, so she didn't want any sort of additional temptation.

When she closed the doors behind them, she turned to face him.

They stared at each other in silence for almost a minute.

Then she finally said, "I meant what I said yesterday. I'm not going to change my mind."

"I know." He took off his mask and then took a step closer to her but almost immediately stepped back again. He clenched his hands at his side. "I'm not here to try to persuade you otherwise."

"Then why are you here?"

"I wanted to say you were right. You were right about everything."

This wasn't at all what she'd expected. She crossed her arms over her chest. "About what?"

"About how I'm not good for you. I..." He cleared his throat. "I've never felt so good as when I'm with you. Not just my body. All of me. All of me felt so good. With you. I... wanted it to last for as long as it could. But that was wrong. That was selfish."

She dropped her eyes, trying to deal with a new surge of feeling at his words. Unable to stop herself, she darted her gaze back up to his face. "It's only selfish if you can't give me anything in return."

"I can't," he said in close to a whisper.

Her eyes dropped again. So did her heart.

"There's something else I need to do. Something more important."

She'd known this almost from the first time she'd met him. He had a different priority. A secret one. Something he was doing here other than winning the Tournament. Whatever it was, was dangerous. *He* was dangerous.

She had no business being so crushed about hearing those words from him now.

He'd made it clear then. He'd made it clear yesterday.

He was making it clear now.

She was the foolish one who kept hoping for something different, based on nothing more than that look she kept imagining to see in his eyes.

"So I need to apologize about yesterday. I was acting on emotion, and it was wrong. I never should have demanded you give me more when I can't... give you everything."

Her throat had completely closed up again, so she just nodded mutely, keeping her eyes on the floor.

"So I came to say I'm sorry." His voice was so gravelly he had to clear it before he added, "And to say goodbye."

She gasped, her eyes flying up to his face. "Goodbye?"

His expression was aching and tender and soft. So incredibly soft. "Yes. Goodbye."

"Where... where are you going?"

"The Tournament is over."

"But the celebrations—"

He gave a shrug, brushing it off like it was nothing. "I'll go to the banquet tonight. That will be it. My... work here is almost over."

"What work?"

"I can't tell you that, Talia."

"Why not? You know I won't tell anyone. I would keep your secrets." She twisted her hands together, suddenly terrified by the look she saw on his face.

Determined.

Doomed.

Final.

"What are you going to do, Desh?"

"What I should have done from the beginning instead of enjoying myself with you."

"What does that mean?" She forgot her resolution to never touch him again and stepped over to grab one of his arms. "Desh, what are you going to do?"

"It doesn't matter."

"It matters to me. What—"

"I'm going to do what I came here to do." Very gently he pulled his arm out of her grip. "What I need to do. Someone has to answer for what's wrong in this world."

She'd heard that note in his voice before, although back then she hadn't known how to understand it. Now she did. A wave of terror slammed into her. "And you think you're the one who has to answer it?"

He stared at her for a long, shuddering moment. "There's no one else who can."

Had she thought through his words and meaning rationally, she would have seen them as illogical, as suspicious, as arrogant. But she didn't think them through.

She just instinctively understood them as true.

"Desh, please don't do anything stupid," she whispered.

"Of course I will," he murmured, leaning over to kiss her just on the corner of her mouth. "That's what I'm here for."

"But—"

He covered her lips with two of his fingers. "I love you, Talia. I never expected anything like it, but I do."

Tears streamed down her cheeks.

He kissed her again. "Goodbye, sweetheart. You've given me joy I've never known before."

She was wracked by waves of grief, so she couldn't speak, she couldn't stop him.

He turned around and walked out of the room.

When she could finally move, she hurried after him. He was already down the hall and through the common room, walking out through the exit to the suite.

She caught up with him in the corridor just outside the entrance. "Desh!"

He turned around at her cry, and she reached him at last. He'd put on his mask before he'd left the playroom, so she couldn't see his expression. She clung to his arm. "Desh, I don't want you to do this."

"I don't have a choice."

"Yes, you do! You could—"

He shook off her arm. "I can't do anything else."

Despite his firm tone, she was going to object again. She was going to argue. She didn't know exactly what Desh was planning to do, but she knew it was stupid, reckless, dangerous.

She knew it was going to get him killed.

He'd told her once that, by the time he was recognized, it would be too late.

Too late felt like it was upon them right now.

But before she could get any more words out, a new voice broke out in the hall. It was male, authoritative, loud. Familiar. "What's going on here?"

She literally jumped. She whirled around to see Marshall, a subcommander of Coalition Special Forces. He was with two guards, and he was heading toward her now in long, sure strides.

"Is he hurting you?" Marshall demanded, turning to glare at Desh, who had lifted a hand to straighten his mask.

"No!" Talia tried to make her voice cool and casual, but didn't really succeed. "No, of course not."

"Why are you crying?"

"I was—" She had absolutely no idea what to say, what excuse she could give for weeping in the hall with Desh like this.

"She was being unreasonable," Desh cut in sharply, in a pitiless voice that wasn't anything like his real self. "So I had to speak harshly to her. Women cry easily."

The words were like physical wounds in her chest. Not because Desh meant them, but because he was trying to protect her by acting like a heartless ass.

Marshall narrowed his eyes as he looked Desh over from top to bottom. "The Tournament is over," he said at last. "Why are you still wearing the mask?"

"Habit."

"Take it off."

Desh didn't move.

Marshall moved his hand to his sidearm. "Do it now."

Very slowly Desh removed his mask.

Talia was holding her breath, but she didn't know why.

Marshall studied Desh's face but obviously didn't know him. "Hold out your arm." He pulled out his scanner and pressed it against Desh's skin.

It would pull up an identity record to match his DNA.

Talia didn't know what Marshall was seeing in the record, but it was obviously not a problem. He frowned but didn't react suspiciously.

"You can leave," Marshall said at last. "But the escorts are protected here. You can't treat them like cheap whores. If you make another one cry, you'll face consequences."

Talia saw a brief struggle on Desh's face, as if he had a problem with what Marshall had said, but he dropped his eyes and murmured, "My mistake. I apologize."

Then he was turning away.

Talia watched his back as he walked away from her, and it occurred to her then that she'd never see him again.

This was it.

He glanced back once, meeting her eyes, before he turned down another hallway.

She was shaking helplessly as she wiped her tears away.

Marshall was still standing beside her. She couldn't let down her guard yet.

"Are you all right?" he asked, turning to face her.

"Yes, yes, of course. He wasn't nice, but he didn't hurt me."

"You shouldn't let men like that bother you. Just don't give them any time."

She nodded. "I won't. Thank you."

Marshall was still frowning thoughtfully in the direction Desh had disappeared in. "How many times have you seen him?"

She almost choked on the tension in her throat. "I... uh, I don't really remember. Several."

She tried to make it vague, but she couldn't lie to him. If Marshall checked, he would easily find out she hadn't told him the truth, and that would be the most dangerous thing she could do.

"He was the one who was talking about those rebellions you looked up a few weeks back, wasn't he?"

She stifled a gasp.

Shit.

Shit, shit, shit, shit, shit.

"N-no. That wasn't him."

Marshall turned his head, studying her face closely. "Why are you trying to protect him?"

"I'm not! I just… I just don't want any trouble."

"You won't get into trouble. You haven't done anything wrong." He reached out to stroke her cheek. "Don't look so scared. It's not your fault if he's up to trouble. I need to check out a few things, but I'll come to find you later."

She swallowed hard and managed to smile. "I'll be waiting."

Marshall left with the other guards, and Talia's knees almost buckled.

He obviously suspected Desh. He was going to check up on him somehow.

Whoever Desh was, he'd obviously managed to create a convincing identity in Coalition records, but there might be some other way for Marshall to find out about him.

What if he found out that Desh was a criminal, that he was here for reasons of his own?

Desh would be immediately arrested, and his sentence would be a prison planet for sure—those were utterly inescapable—rather than the slightly easier sentence of a planet dump.

Desh—her handsome, gentle Desh—stuck in a hellhole prison until he died.

She couldn't stand for that to happen. She could barely even process the thought in her mind.

But how was she supposed to stop it from happening?

Desh had made it clear that things were over between them, and that was obviously for the best. She had to think about herself. She had to protect herself.

Any further involvement with Desh would only put her in very real danger.

Desh didn't want her help anyway.

Plus there was absolutely nothing she could do.

Confused and trembling and almost numb with so much emotion, Talia went back into the leisure suite.

She couldn't face the curious looks of Breann and the others, so she kept walking through the common room, turning down a hall that led to Jenelle's room.

Jenelle invited her in at her buzz, and Talia stepped in to the small, pretty bedroom—that had once been the pinnacle of Talia's ambitions.

"What's wrong?" Jenelle asked urgently, obviously seeing signs of distress on Talia's face.

Talia sank into a chair. "I... I don't know. Desh is in trouble, I think."

"Of course he's in trouble. I knew something was up with him. I told you to stay away from him."

"I know you did." She slumped her shoulders and admitted, "He said goodbye. He doesn't want to see me again."

Jenelle's face was sympathetic, but she shook her head. "Didn't I tell you that would happen?"

"Yes. You did."

"But you fell for him anyway." It wasn't a question.

Talia closed her eyes. "Yes. I'm afraid I did."

Jenelle was silent for a long time before she said, "Well, don't beat yourself up about it."

Surprised, Talia shot a quick look at her. "You've been warning me for weeks now."

"I know I have. But wise warnings don't have a chance of making a dent when your heart gets in the way." Jenelle was smiling poignantly. "It happens to all of us. You'll get over it."

More confused than ever, Talia asked slowly, "It happens to all of us?"

"Well, most of us. Eventually. There's always one of our partners we like too much, who we start to get hopes about."

"It happened to you?"

"Why do you look so surprised?"

"I don't know," Talia admitted. "You just always seem too... cool and in control, keeping things in perspective."

"Now I am, yes. I wasn't always this way."

"You let yourself hope in someone?"

"Yes." Jenelle's smile faded, and she stared at Talia blindly for a moment. "I did. I was disappointed. All of us were. We're escorts. We're not potential lifetime partners. The sooner you accept this, the better off you'll be. No matter what you dream about, men are never going to see you in any other way."

Talia sat motionless, her mind racing.

Desh had seen her differently.

He'd seen her as more than a body.

She was convinced of it.

"Don't try to persuade yourself that some silly, romanticized version of the world is the true one," Jenelle added, sounding almost tired. "I can see on your face what's happening in your mind, and I'm telling you now it will end in more heartache. Men will always be men. They might talk pretty for a while, but in the end they'll just take what they want from us."

"Not all men—"

"Yes, all men! The ones who don't just don't have the power to do it. But give them the power, and they'll do the exact same thing. All this civilized equality is nothing but a pretense. You've been here long enough. You should know that by now. Sex is about power, and those with power use it against everyone else. That's the world that we live in. So take any power you have, and make the best of it, like everyone else."

Talia stared at her friend, her mentor, shocked and saddened by the bitterness in her voice.

The bitterness she understood though.

Jenelle might be a favorite of a powerful man. She might have her own room and privileges that Talia had only dreamed of.

But that was all Jenelle knew.

That was all she had to hope for.

Talia knew there was more now.

There was more, better, deeper.

She was more, better, deeper than the sex object she'd been raised to become.

And a life that was more, better, deeper was what she wanted.

Even if it meant taking risks.

Even if it meant risking everything.

She finally understood what motivated all the heroes in her favorite stories, that queen who should have been only a sex object but who had managed to save her people.

Some things were worth more than safety.

And Talia's world was different now. And she'd rather be dead than live an empty, barren existence—the life she'd lived for so long now.

She didn't want it anymore.

She wanted... something else.

She wanted to *be* something else.

She was a full human being with a soul and a free will, and she was going to use it to make the decisions she wanted to make in her life.

"What's the matter?" Jenelle asked, evidently seeing something on Talia's face.

Talia shook her head fiercely. "Nothing. It's nothing."

Jenelle clearly didn't believe her. "Don't do anything stupid, Talia. Promise me you won't do anything stupid. One man isn't worth it. He's just not worth it."

Talia stood up and met her friend's eyes. "It's not about him."

For a long stretch of time, Jenelle didn't do anything. Didn't speak. Didn't move a muscle.

Then she finally gave a very slight nod.

As if she understood.

With a rush of feeling, Talia stepped over to take Jenelle's hand. "Thank you," she said. "For everything."

Jenelle nodded again, something like loss in her eyes.

Talia turned to leave. She couldn't waste any more time, now that she'd made her decision.

She extended her arm as she stepped away until her hand finally slipped out of Jenelle's grasp.

Then she hurried.

Down the hall. Through the common room. Out to the main corridors. To the guest wing. To Desh's room.

She buzzed and kept buzzing until the doors slid open.

Desh was coming out of the bathroom, looking sleek and handsome and determined in formal attire.

He was going to the banquet tonight.

He was almost on his way.

"Talia," he said, his blue eyes widening. "What are you doing—"

"You need to get out of here. You need to leave right away!"

"What are you talking about? I'm going—"

"You can't go to the banquet. Marshall suspects you. He said he was going to check up on you. He'll find out who you are and whatever you're hiding, and he'll arrest you. He'll catch you, Desh!"

He took in her urgent flurry of words, and then his expression settled into that doomed one she'd seen on his face more than once. "It doesn't matter," he said softly. "It will be too late then."

"What? *What*? Desh, please!"

"You shouldn't be here. I know what I'm doing."

She grabbed for him, clutching at the front of his jacket. "Desh, please just get out of here."

"Talia, I can't. I told you. I have something to do that's more important." Despite his words, his eyes were lost and aching.

Heartbreaking.

"But I'm telling you that you're not going to be able to do whatever it is you want to do. Marshall isn't going to let you."

"He won't be able to stop me. I just need to make it to the banquet tonight."

She dropped her hands, growing still as she processed his words. "What happens at the banquet?"

"I'm finally in the same room as the High Director."

"But what does that have to do—"

"It's what I'm here for. I can finally take off my mask."

He was scaring her now, sounding cold, ruthless. "Will he... will he recognize you?"

"Oh yes," Desh breathed.

"But then he'll know you're a criminal! The fake record won't mean anything. You'll get arrested and not be able to do anything."

"All I need is a few seconds." He cleared his throat, suddenly looking more like himself. "Talia, please, you need to leave. You're putting yourself in danger by being here, and it's making it harder for me to do what I need to do. I can't let you tempt me to be... soft."

"Soft?" Her mind was finally putting the pieces together. She had all the pieces she needed now. "Desh, what are you planning to do? You think you're going to... going to... kill him?"

Desh didn't answer.

He didn't need to.

She saw the answer on his face.

She almost choked. "You came here to kill the High Director?"

"Yes," he said very softly, no expression at all on his face. "Somebody has to. He has to answer for everything he's done."

"That was your plan all along? It's some sort of rebellion you're part of?"

He shook his head and licked his lips before he answered. "It's no rebellion. It's only me. It's just… an answer."

"But it's a terrible answer! They'll kill you! They'll *kill* you, Desh!"

Very slowly he turned his eyes to meet hers. "Some things are more important. This is my answer."

The words nearly knocked her down.

Desh added, very softly, "My life was over a long time ago."

That brought her back. She nearly snapped her teeth as she bit out, "You idiot! You're still trying to punish yourself, to suffer because you think you don't deserve to be happy."

"I can't be happy. I can't. Not in a world that's gone so wrong. I need to answer it."

She understood him. She believed him. But she also knew something else. "Then *answer* it! Answer it for real! Not like this. What exactly do you think this is going to accomplish? Even if you do manage to kill him, nothing will change. It will all be for nothing. And you know it. You know it! This isn't a mission. It isn't a real answer. It's a suicide. It's a suicide that you've been drawing out for years now."

His expression flickered just slightly.

She sucked in a sharp breath. "You know it. You already know it. You're not a heartless assassin, Desh. You're not like that. You're—"

"I'm not weak," he cut in with a biting tone.

She reached out to take his face in her hands. "Of course you're not weak. You're so strong. But it's your heart that's the strongest thing. You're going to get to that banquet and stand before the High Director, and you're not going to be able to do it. No matter how much you want to, no matter how much you hate him, you're never going to be able to kill a man in cold blood. You know it. And you know you're going to die in the process. All to prove what? Prove that you're not weak? Prove that someone needs to do something to fix things?"

She was almost crying again, but she was too filled with anger and feeling and outrage to do so. The words kept pouring out. "So then fix things. Fix things for real. Do something that means something instead of throwing your life away on a suicide mission that won't accomplish anything."

Desh's expression was flickering even more, and she knew he was hearing her. The cold hardness she'd sensed in him the moment before was softening into the man he really was. "Talia, sweetheart, there's nothing else I can do," he murmured hoarsely.

"Yes, there is. There is! If you're brave enough to do the harder thing. All those stories I read about worlds being made better, all of them start in exactly the same way. One person decides to do what's right instead of what's easy. One person throws off the shackles of fate and makes a different decision. One person goes against the current of the rest of the world and changes the direction of the tide. Why can't that person be you? If you go to that banquet tonight, you won't be doing what's brave, what's strong. You'll be submitting to fate, to everything that's wrong in the world. You're better than that. You're stronger than that, Desh. You've always felt this calling to answer what's wrong in the world. I think you've felt that for a reason." She paused when she ran out of breath and then added hoarsely, "So why can't the one person who changes everything be you?"

His face twisted with emotion, and his eyes were glimmering with something that looked like tears. He gave her a poignant smile. "Because it's too late."

She made a little sob. "No, it's not, Desh! Why do you keep believing that?"

He released a soft huff of amusement. "That's not what I mean, sweetheart. I mean someone has already done what's right in the face of all that's wrong. Someone has already taken the first step to change everything. And that person is you."

She sobbed for real then, her hands coming up to cover her face briefly. When she lowered them, Desh was smiling at her.

Desh.

Her Desh.

The real man.

Not the hardened warrior he'd tried to be for so long.

"So what will you do?" she asked, a rush of excitement filling her like nothing she'd ever experienced before. "You need to get out of here right away."

"I'm not going anywhere without you."

She jerked in surprise. "But you said we… we didn't have a future."

"I said that because I didn't believe *I* had a future. If I do something else, if I don't… do what I planned, then I don't want to do it without you."

"So you…" She was almost strangling on a different kind of tension in her throat. "So you want me to come with you?"

He reached out for her hand. "I told you I loved you. Didn't you understand what that means?"

She swayed on her feet, opening her mouth to answer, to try to express everything she was feeling.

But she didn't have the chance.

The doors to Desh's room slid open without warning, and two guards stood in the hall outside them.

Two guards.

And Marshall.

Talia's vision whited out in fear.

Marshall's face reflected shock when he saw Talia in Desh's room. "What are you doing here?" he demanded. "He's a criminal. I told you I was— Are you *helping* him?" He sounded angry, horrified.

Talia tried to make herself answer, tried to think of any sort of excuse or justification for her presence here.

There was none.

She was guilty, and Marshall would know it now.

Just on the verge of finding freedom for the first time in her life, she was going to be arrested and convicted of aiding and abetting a criminal.

This was the Coalition.

Her sentence would be just as harsh as Desh's was.

Desh had moved closer to her, and his arm had gone around her. She gasped when she felt something pressing into her back.

It was a weapon.

She couldn't see what kind, but it was sharp. A knife or something like it.

"You think a whore would have helped me willingly?" Desh asked in that nasty voice that wasn't at all like him. "She didn't have a choice. Just like you don't have a choice right now. Let me go, or I'm going to kill her."

Marshall laughed. He actually laughed. "You think the life of an escort is enough to stop us from arresting you? I did a facial recognition search on you. You know there's security cameras all through the Residence, don't you? You took off your mask earlier, so I ran a search. I don't know how you changed your identity record, but I know who you are. I know you were arrested twelve years ago for sedition. And I know who your father is. We're taking you to the Headquarters right now. Kill the girl if you want to. It's not going to stop us."

He meant it. Marshall really didn't care if Desh killed her.

She was nothing but an object to him.

That was all she'd ever been.

She wasn't an object to Desh though. He knew her as human. He loved her as human. And he was doing what he could to protect her right now.

He pushed her away from him, causing her to stumble and fall against the table, knocking over a couple of glasses and the silver bowl that had held the grapes and landing on the med device she'd been using on Desh after his fights to heal his injuries.

"Much good you turned out to be, whore," Desh snapped at her. He was doing a good job at convincing Marshall that she was absolutely meaningless to him.

It was the only way she could remain safe.

Talia started to cry. She couldn't help it, but maybe Marshall would believe it was because Desh had used her so roughly. She was still draped over the table, and as she stood up, she palmed the med device and slipped it into her pocket.

Other than the knife in Desh's hand, the med device was the only thing in the room that could be used as a weapon.

She'd barely pulled her hand free of her pocket when Marshall turned to look at her, and she covered by using her sleeve to wipe the tears off her face.

"If you'd come to me the first time he tried to use you," Marshall told her, looking annoyed and impatient, "you wouldn't have ended up getting hurt."

Evidently believing he'd said all he needed to say to her, Marshall turned to the other guards. "Cuff him, and get moving. There's a shuttle waiting to take him to Headquarters."

Talia watched through her tears as Desh was put into cuffs. He didn't fight back, and she was convinced it was because he didn't want to put her in any more danger. When he was shoved forward toward the door, Marshall said to him, "I wonder what the High Director will say when he discovers I've arrested his traitorous son who's supposed to be dead."

Talia froze as the words registered in her mind.

She didn't even know the High Director had a son.

Apparently he did.

And apparently that son was Desh.

All the missing pieces fell into place with that one detail, Desh's whole life laying out in crystal clarity in her mind.

Now she understood that Desh's plan here was even more of a suicide mission than she'd initially believed.

Desh was a good man.

He would always be a good man.

If he couldn't kill just any man in cold blood, he never would have been able to kill his father.

The fact that he'd believed he could just showed how far anger and desperation had taken him.

He would die now.

Capital punishment might be outlawed by the Coalition as a barbaric custom, not befitting a civilized society that had progressed so far, but there were plenty of ways around it.

One way or another, Desh would die for what he'd done.

And Talia simply couldn't let that happen.

She was just one girl. A leisure escort. Not even worthy of being a legitimate hostage.

And all she had was a medical device in her pocket.

She had no idea what she could do to stop it.

EIGHT

Talia might have had a chance—not a good one, but a chance—had they left her in Desh's room when they left, as she assumed they would.

Marshall and the guards appeared to believe what Desh had wanted them to believe. That he'd used Talia and threatened her to get her to help him.

She thought they would take him to the shuttle and leave her alone to return to the leisure suite, appropriately chastened for not reporting Desh immediately the way she should have but facing no further consequences.

Once they left, she would have a very small opportunity of doing something to help. No one would be watching her. She could do... something.

But before he left the room, Marshall turned to glance at her over his shoulder. "You better come along."

Talia jerked in surprise. "But why?" She didn't have to pretend that her voice was weak and trembling. "Am I... am I in trouble?"

"No, but we need to get the whole story from him, and you can fill in some of the gaps."

"The whore doesn't know anything," Desh snarled. "Don't waste your time."

"I'm not a whore," she said, shrinking away from him, her mind racing as she tried to figure out what was best for her to say, how was best for her to act. "And you deserve everything you'll get."

"I'll decide what's a waste of my time," Marshall said coolly, shaking his head at Desh. Then he turned to Talia. "You better come along."

She stared at him with wide, scared eyes.

He rolled his eyes as if he were getting tired of this whole situation. "You're not in trouble as long as you tell us everything we want to know."

"Is he really..." She shrunk away from Desh again, acting like she was turning to Marshall for protection. "Is he really the High Director's son?"

"I think so. The facial recognition matches. But I need to do more research, and I need to get him to talk. We've got drugs that will make him tell us everything at Headquarters. And if that doesn't work, we have other methods of interrogations. We'll get the whole story." Marshall turned stone-cold eyes on Desh. "And then we can tell the High Director that his long-lost son has been found. It will be quite the family reunion."

Talia shuddered in terror, but she still had a role to play. "You haven't told the High Director yet?"

"No. I'm not that foolish. You don't approach the High Director until you have all the answers to questions he might ask. Now get moving. You can ride with us in the shuttle over to Headquarters."

Talia nodded and dropped her eyes, walking beside Marshall down the corridor.

Desh was cuffed. The two guards were armed, as was Marshall.

There was absolutely nothing she could do to get away from them, much less get Desh away.

And even if she somehow managed, she'd never be able to leave the Residence. All entrances and docking bays were monitored. An escort would never be able to leave without prior permission.

She was trapped here, as much as she would have been trapped on a prison planet.

She didn't want to leave without Desh anyway.

She searched her mind as they walked, but no miraculous plan of escape came to her. So she ended up on the shuttle with no clear idea what to do. She was sitting across from Desh and one of the guards. The other guard was piloting, and Marshall was in the copilot seat.

She listened as they communicated with the guard tower for the Residence, explaining they were on their way to the Coalition Security Headquarters, which orbited Earth just like the Residence.

She met Desh's eyes across the shuttle, hoping for a brilliant plan for escape.

He gave his head the slightest shake.

He didn't want her to do anything.

He was clearly telling her not to.

He was scared for her. She could see it in his eyes.

He wasn't scared for himself.

He was scared for *her*.

He'd rather go to his death than put her at even the slightest risk.

But he didn't understand that she felt exactly the same way.

She didn't want to live without him either.

When the shuttle took off, she slipped her hand into her pocket.

She still had the med device. It wasn't much of a weapon, but it was something. It would only work if she could press it against someone's skin though. It would do her no good at all at a distance. Very carefully she felt around on it until she was able to switch the settings to knock someone unconscious.

Desh's eyes widened. He could see she was doing something, but he must not know what she was doing.

When the guard next to him turned his head in her direction, Desh said quickly, "Why didn't we leave the whore back where she belongs?"

Marshall turned his seat around to face Desh. He was frowning thoughtfully. "Why are you so obsessed with her?"

Talia felt a chill run down her spine.

"I'm not obsessed. I don't give a fuck about her." Desh was giving an impressive performance of being arrogant and disinterested.

But Marshall wasn't a stupid man. His expression had changed. "You're trying to protect her."

"I'm not doing anything like—"

"You are," Marshall breathed, his eyes turning over to Talia. "You fell for the bitch."

Desh made a growling sound, and Talia rose to her feet instinctively.

Marshall got up too, stepping over and taking her chin in his hand with a calculating expression. "Have you been lying to me the whole time then? Well, you'll still be of use to me. If you mean something to him, we can get him to talk by hurting you."

She jerked her head away from his hand, but he just grabbed it again. More roughly. He added very nastily, "Maybe I'll even show him how you really like to be fucked."

Desh tackled Marshall.

He literally tackled him, launching himself at the other man despite his cuffs and despite the small space on the shuttle.

When the two men went down in a tumble of arms and legs, Talia gave a little squeal. But she had sense enough to pull the med device out of her pocket and hold it against the back of the guard's neck, who had jumped to his feet to help Marshall.

The guard went down in less than ten seconds, falling to the floor completely unconscious.

This med device was really something.

Desh and Marshall were grappling on the floor, so Talia ran over to the pilot seat, where the other guard had reached toward a communicator.

He was probably going to call for help.

Talia used the med device on the back of his neck before he could, and he fell limply against the seat.

When she whirled around, Desh was on top of Marshall, holding his forearms against the other man's throat, despite the cuffs.

Marshall was strong and well trained, but Desh had trained with The Master on Mel Tana for years. Cuffs weren't enough to hold him back.

"Someone needs to fly the shuttle, and I don't know how," Talia said, her heart beating so fast it was almost strangling her. She leaned over and held the med device against Marshall's arm. "So let's just knock him out."

When Marshall went limp, Desh hauled himself to his feet, flushed and panting and a new kind of fire smoldering in his eyes. He reached out for her before he remembered he was still cuffed.

He scowled down at his bound hands.

Talia laughed a little hysterically and reached into Marshall's pocket for the cuff release. When she pressed it, the cuffs opened and Desh tossed them onto the floor.

He went over to the pilot's seat, dragged the unconscious guard out of the chair, and then sat down himself.

The shuttle was on course toward Headquarters, but Desh pressed a few buttons and steered them in a different direction.

Talia stood where she was, hugging herself tightly. "We can't go very far in this shuttle."

"We'll need to dump it as soon as possible and find another vehicle."

"Will they know to chase us right away?"

"I don't know. It depends on how much he told Headquarters. It sounded like he was waiting for more information before he filled those in command in, and that would give us an advantage. They won't know who I am or know that we're a threat until we're pretty far away." He glanced behind him at the unconscious men. "How long will they be out for?"

"I don't really know." Getting nervous, she checked the small screen of the med device. "Oh here, you can set it for a specific amount of time. The most is four hours." She ran the device at that setting over each of the unconscious men in the shuttle. "That will give us a little time. We don't want them waking up yet. Do you..." She had to pause to catch her breath. "Do you think we can actually do this? Get away?"

Desh turned his head and smiled at her, the fondness in his eyes making her heart melt. "He apparently hadn't told everyone who I was yet, so it might be possible, if we can get far enough away before the time they regain consciousness. You're amazing. Do you know that?"

She smiled back at him, feeling something different, something new. Something she recognized as joy.

She wasn't sure she'd ever really felt it before.

She said, "I didn't know it until I met you."

~

Forty-eight hours later, Talia fell into bed, completely exhausted but finally feeling safe and clean.

They'd taken the shuttle to the Moon, and there they'd knocked the guards out again for four additional hours before they'd dumped the shuttle. They'd rented a transport and put as much distance between them and the Earth as they could before they'd switched vehicles again.

In the past two days, they'd swapped vehicles five times. Then Desh had paid a visit to an old acquaintance of his who'd helped them both wipe their old identities and create new ones.

They'd seen no signs of pursuit, so they were as safe as they were likely to get as they finally arrived on a mostly undeveloped planet, the one where Desh's friends lived. The place he'd said he go if he could go anywhere in the world.

Talia was too tired to interact much with their hosts, a friendly, attractive couple who lived in a big, sprawling house next to vineyards.

Vineyards.

She did manage to notice that much.

They were so bedraggled and exhausted that they'd gone straight to bed after a bite to eat and some brief conversation.

Talia was still having trouble keeping up with it all, but this much she'd managed to process.

They'd gotten away.

They were safe, at least for the moment.

They were on the planet where his friend from the cave had also moved with her family.

And Talia's life would never be the same again.

She was no longer an escort.

She was Desh's partner now—unless he decided to change his mind.

She didn't think he would.

She'd taken a shower first while he was still talking to the couple who owned the house, so she was lying in bed, clean and happy and comfortable, when he got out of the shower himself.

He was naked except for a towel, and he stood next to the bed, gazing down at her.

"If you're even thinking about telling me that you made a mistake or that you don't want me around anymore," she said, scowling at him, "then I'm going to have to beat you up."

He chuckled and sat down on the edge of the bed, reaching to take her hand. "I don't want you to beat me up, so I wouldn't dream of telling you such a thing. I'm just trying to…" He trailed off, shaking his head. "I'm trying to convince myself that all this is real."

"Why wouldn't it be real?"

"Because I thought I'd be dead," he admitted softly. "By now, I thought I'd already be dead. I kept imagining myself finally confronting my father, proving that I wasn't as weak as he'd always made me feel, proving that I will always stand against his oppression and cruel ambition. I'd be dead almost immediately. Of course, I would be killed as soon as he knew who I was. But I would have… proven something to him. At least made a gesture toward what I believe in before the end."

She squeezed his hand and then pulled him down toward her until he was stretched out on the bed beside her. "It would have been a futile gesture. Isn't it better this way?"

He pulled her hand up so he could kiss her knuckles. "It's better because I'm here with you. But it's also going to be a lot harder. I was serious before, back on the Residence, when I said I need to do something. I… Part of me would love to set up a home here on this planet, live a life that's safe and comfortable and filled with…" He shook his head again. "But I can't. I'm so sorry, sweetheart, but I can't."

She gave him a shaky smile. "I know you can't. I never thought you would. And part of me might like the idea of that kind of life too, but I'd rather be with the man you really are, doing what you need to do. The truth is maybe I need to do it too."

His expression softened, and he was still holding her hand up near his mouth. He kissed it again. Then he licked his lips, clearly thinking things through.

"I'll need to travel around," he said at last.

She nodded. She'd already thought that far ahead. She'd been planning things out in her mind for years now. She had more ideas than most. "There are all those little rebellions going on. If anything is ever going to get to the point of threatening the Coalition, someone needs to start uniting them. The son of the High Director might have a real chance of doing that. If anyone can."

Desh let out a long breath. "That's what I was thinking too. We can't… we can't do anything until we know what we have to work with. I don't know how long it will take. But Hall and Kyla say that you can stay here for however long it—"

"No!" she burst out. "What are you talking about? I'm not going to stay here."

"But it's safe here. And whatever I'm doing, wherever I'm going, it's not going to be safe."

"I don't care! I'm not going to do it. I'm done with being a pretty object to be taken out whenever a man feels like it."

"Sweetheart, no! I'd never think you were—"

"I know you don't think about me that way, but that's how I would feel. If you left me here, that's how I would feel. I want to go with you. I think I can help. I don't know how, but I have some good ideas. And I think... I think you need me."

"I do need you." He pressed another kiss on her hand, this time on her open palm. "But I'd rather you be safe."

She shook her head. "Desh, how long do you think it's going to be before your father figures out what you're doing?"

"I... I don't know. But he will eventually."

"And when he does, he's going to be looking for any kind of weakness in you. He's going to be searching for any way he can hurt you. How long do you think it will take for him to realize that you have someone... someone special to you? He'll eventually find me here, and then your friends will be in danger too. This lovely planet will be destroyed just like that other world you loved. I'm not going to be safe anywhere, Desh, so I'm going to stay with you."

He was quiet for a long time. Then he finally nodded. "I do need you. You know that, don't you?"

"Yes. I know it."

"I'll never be able to do this without you."

"Well, you have me." She scooted a little closer to him. "And I have you. So it seems a pretty fair deal to me."

"Damn, I love you so much, Talia."

She gave him a wobbly smile. "I love you too."

"Do you?"

She giggled and moved over on top of him. "Yes, I love you. Didn't you know that already?"

"Well. I was hoping." He slid his hands down to her hips, holding her against him. She could feel him growing hard against her lower belly.

Her pussy clenched in response, and she rubbed herself against him.

He groaned and took her head in both hands to pull her down into a kiss.

They kissed for a long time, gently, leisurely, so sweetly. Her body was washed with waves of pleasure and feeling—too deep to put into words. She was fully aroused—and so was he—when she finally broke the kiss and straightened up so she could untie her tunic.

She was straddling his hips, and he stared up at her hotly as she pulled the fabric away to bare her body and then let the tunic slip off her shoulders.

His hips bucked up a few times in jerky little moves, as if he were too turned on to hold himself still.

She loved that about him. Loved that he was so uncontrolled, so unpracticed, so genuine.

She'd never known a man could be like that before, open himself up so completely, be with her for real.

With a slow smile, she opened the towel he had wrapped around his hips and pulled out his hard cock. He groaned as she stroked him gently, and then he lifted his hands to fondle her breasts.

She gasped and arched in pleasure and then gasped again when one of his hands slid down to play with her wet pussy.

He caressed her like that until she came in a fast rush, biting her lip hard to stifle the cry of pleasure. Then she lifted herself up on her knees and lined herself up on his cock, lowering her hips until she sheathed him with her pussy.

"Fuck, sweetheart," he rasped, holding handfuls of her bottom in his big hands. "Fuck, you feel so good. How do you do this to me every time?"

She started to ride him, filled with him completely, so fully, so tightly that there was nothing in the world left for her to need. He gazed up at her, awe and adoration in his eyes as she moved.

He wasn't taking from her. He was giving; he was loving her. And so she was able to give back. She was able to love too.

It didn't take very long for another climax to tighten at her center, and it was a good thing too because he wasn't going to last very long. He was grunting softly as his hips rocked beneath her, growing faster, more urgent, less controlled.

She rode him hard until an orgasm broke inside her, and as her pussy clamped down around him, he choked on a stifled cry of completion. His body jerked through the spasms, and his face transformed in a wave of pure pleasure, contentment.

Release.

He'd lived so long without ever allowing himself such a thing.

And now he had it.

She could give it to him.

It made her so incredibly happy.

She fell down on top of him, sated and relaxed, and he wrapped his strong arms around her.

"I love you, sweetheart," he murmured into her hair.

She wasn't wearing a ponytail, and her long hair was falling down all around them both. The freedom was unfamiliar.

And she loved it.

"I love you too," she said. "And now I'm very tired, so maybe we can save any more conversation until tomorrow morning."

He chuckled and stroked her hair, her back. "Sounds good to me."

After a minute, she rolled off him and snuggled up at his side. He pulled the covers up over both of them.

It took only a few minutes for her to fall asleep, and Desh was asleep before she was.

It was the best night's sleep she'd ever had.

~

They slept in late the following morning, and when they did wake up, they took it easy, eating a leisurely breakfast, chatting with Hall, handsome and charismatic, and his quiet wife Kyla, and then taking a long walk together, during which they started to make plans for the next few months of their lives.

Talia enjoyed it, more than she could remember enjoying anything. She liked Hall and Kyla, and she loved walking through their vineyards, sampling a number of different grapes. She knew they wouldn't have very long here on this planet that seemed so cut off from the rest of the universe, but she loved that such a place existed.

For dinner, Hall and Kyla invited some friends over. Two couples and their children, who also knew Desh.

One of the women was the friend he'd had when he'd lived on that primitive planet. Her name was Lenna, and she was pretty and blond and intelligent and immediately likable. Her husband, Rone, was big and strong and handsome with his hair in a long, sleek braid down his back. He didn't say much, and when he did speak, it was with an accent. He had a kind smile, though, and an earnest, searching gaze.

Desh had told her about him, about how until last year he'd never known the rest of the universe even existed. She couldn't imagine how someone could go through that sort of transition, and she hated that he'd been forced into it.

Rone and Lenna had two daughters and a son. The transition had been less hard on the children.

The other family who came over was a large, intimidating man named Cain who didn't seem all that friendly and his wife, Riana, who was much more approachable. They had a son and a daughter, just a little older than Rone and Lenna's children.

They all ate outside in the sunshine, and Talia could tell that Desh was genuinely glad to spend time with his friends, catching up on their lives and telling them about his.

She was happy that he could have this, even though they both knew they couldn't stay here long.

After dinner, Rone stayed outside to play with the children, and the rest of them helped bring the dishes into the kitchen.

Wanting to be useful, Talia found the half-empty bottle of wine they'd been drinking—crisp and delicious and better than any replicated wine she'd ever tasted—and went around filling up people's glasses.

When she returned the wine to the counter, she looked around and saw that everyone was looking at Desh.

Desh was obviously aware of it too. "What's going on?" he asked, eyeing the people around him.

Talia went over to stand beside him, and he reached out to take her hand in his.

Hall was one of those men to whom words and laughter came easily. It was impossible not to like him. He was leaning against the wall, a glass of wine in his hand. He said, "I've been telling the others about your plans."

"Oh." Desh looked around, clearly trying to read the others' expressions. "I'll understand if you think it's crazy."

"No one thinks it's crazy," Hall said. His green eyes were uncharacteristically sober.

Lenna met Desh's eyes and gave him a little nod. She was sitting in a chair near the window.

Talia could feel Desh relax slightly. Clearly his friends' opinions meant something to him. "Good," he said. "I'm glad."

"You're going to need help," Hall added.

"I know." Desh shifted slightly, although he hadn't let go of Talia's hand. "That's my first step. I need to... see how much support there is."

"And it never occurred to you to first see what support you had right here?" Hall's voice was mild, uninflected.

Desh frowned. "I know you all will give me moral support, but what else—"

"What else?" Hall interrupted. "You're really asking us that? You know what I can do, right?"

"Yes," Desh said slowly "I know."

Talia only knew what he was talking about because he'd explained it to her this morning. Hall was some kind of empath who could sense other people's emotions when he touched them and even turn those feelings around, easing pain and anxiety or creating feelings that weren't there.

"And you can't think of any use that gift could be to you, given what you're trying to do?" Hall had arched his eyebrows very slightly.

Desh blinked. "Sure, it might be useful, but you live here, and we're going to have to be traveling around, and—"

"And I'm not capable of traveling too?"

Desh's hand clenched harder around Talia's, but his face was perfectly composed. "What are you saying?"

"I'm saying you need me. You're going to need to know very quickly who you can trust, and I'll be able to tell you that. You need me. So I'm going with you."

"What? No!" Desh's expression was visibly upset, shocked. "I would never ask you to—"

"You don't seem to understand what it is you're going to be doing. You have to ask people to help you. And you have to let them when they offer." If anything, Hall looked faintly amused. "You're never going to get anywhere if you don't."

"But you all are safe here." Desh looked from Hall to Kyla, who was sitting in a chair at the kitchen table. "You're happy. I don't know how long this is going to take. You'd leave Kyla indefinitely like that?"

"No. Of course not. I'd never leave her behind. Kyla is going to come too."

"I can't help like Hall can," Kyla said softly. "I don't have his gift. But I'm sure there's something I can do to help."

"But... but you'll have to give up your life, for who knows how long." Desh was searching the other faces in the room and holding Talia's hand very tightly. "You have a good life here. Your vineyard. I'd never ask you to give all that up. You'd just... Why would you leave?"

"Sometimes it's enough. To live well, to love deeply, to shape something good, something beautiful, even if the rest of the world isn't what it should be." Hall was speaking softly, and his eyes dropped to the glass of wine in his hand. Wine he'd made with his own hands. "Sometimes that's enough to answer what's wrong in the world. But sometimes it's not." He looked up to meet Desh's eyes. "Sometimes you have to do more. Sometimes you have to rise up and meet it."

The words lingered in the silence of the kitchen for a long time, and they made shivers run up and down Talia's spine.

Hall continued, "I know that's what you and Talia are trying to do. You have to let Kyla and I do it too."

Desh swallowed so hard she could see it in his throat. Then he gave a brief nod. "Thank you. I will need your help, so I'll take it."

Turning his head, Desh met Talia's eyes. She gave him a little smile, feeling emotional, almost teary.

She didn't know these people the way Desh did, but even she could feel the ache of what they'd be leaving behind.

"You're going to need more than Hall before it's all over," Lenna said from where she was sitting.

Desh stiffened. "Don't even think of trying to come too," he said. He glanced out the window where Rone was playing with the children in the yard. "After everything that happened to you and Rone, you can't…"

Lenna gave a little shrug and a smile that was slightly wobbly. "No. I'm not coming with you right away. But I'm a pilot. A good one. And you're going to need good pilots before the end. You know you will."

Desh nodded very slowly.

"So when you need me, I'll be there."

"Lenna, I wish you wouldn't. You need more time to settle. It's safe here, and—"

"And how long do you think it's going to stay safe here?" Lenna broke in. "You think they'll never get around to this planet? They destroyed our old world. They took that away from us. Not even to be cruel. They did it just because they could. And that was too wrong. You know it was too wrong." She looked back out the window at her husband, who was laughing and tossing their little boy up into the air.

He looked happy right now, but Talia could only imagine what he'd been through.

Talia had to wipe away a tear, and she saw Kyla doing the same thing.

Desh's voice was rough and broken as he said, "I know it was. I know, Lenna."

"So I can't just hide away anymore. I'm not going to—not if there's something else I can do. You and Talia have made a choice in this, and you have to let the rest of us make a choice too. It's going to be a while—probably years—but I'll be ready for whenever you need me. I'm a good pilot. Cain is too. And there isn't a better mechanic than Cain."

Everyone turned to look at Cain, who was sitting next to his wife at the kitchen table with an utterly stoic expression. At Lenna's words, he gave a brief nod.

Desh's mouth twisted. "I do need help. I know I do. And later I'm sure what we'll need is pilots. But I hate for you all to leave your homes here. To risk your lives. You... you have children."

Lenna shook her head, and Cain finally spoke in his gruff voice. "Our children will have to live in this universe after we are gone. If we can make it better for them, then that's what we have to do."

Desh's hand was shaking in her grip, and Talia squeezed it, trying to encourage him. "We're not at that point yet, Desh," she murmured.

163

He stared at her almost helplessly.

She leaned over to kiss him. "When we are at that point, you'll be ready. I know you will."

He let out a shaky breath. "Okay. Okay. Thank you. All of you. I don't know… I don't know what to say."

"Maybe you can start by telling us your plans for the first steps," Hall said, his light, polished voice breaking the tension and bringing them all back to more normal interaction, much to Talia's relief. "We might have some ideas that can help you."

So they talked for several hours that evening, and together they put together what Talia thought was a very good plan to begin a rebellion.

It wasn't like all those stories she'd read. It was real and tedious and achingly hard. And it would probably take years.

Yet it was exactly like those stories.

One person made a decision, made a hard choice. And then other people made choices as well.

And sometimes it led to suffering. Much would be lost. Even lives.

Always lives.

But in doing so, something else was gained, something too precious to be won easily or achieved without great cost.

And eventually as one person chose good after another, the world could be changed.

Even her world.

It was what she'd always dreamed of.

She'd never known—even a few months ago—that dreams could ever come true.

But her life had already transformed.

And now she believed her world could too.

EPILOGUE

Talia wiped perspiration off her forehead with her forearm.

She'd just unloaded a dozen bags of feed from a transport, and now the huge bags were stacked neatly against the wall in the barn.

Cain and Riana's ranch was old school. They had some equipment, but most of the work was still done by hand. Talia had grown up working around the house with her mother, but she'd never done this kind of manual labor until the past two years.

She kind of liked the feeling of accomplishment, even though her body was sore.

For the past year, she'd been on and off this planet fairly often, ever since they'd taken control of all the solar systems in this corner of what was formerly Coalition space. The entire year before that she and Desh hadn't been able to risk any visits to this planet for fear of calling it to the Coalition's attention.

It had been two years now since Desh had made his decision to organize a rebellion.

For the first ten months, nothing seemed to have happened. She and Desh with Hall and Kyla had traveled through much of Coalition space, finding support, discovering allies, and organizing resources.

Their first real move had been dramatic, coordinated uprisings on eighteen different planets at the same time. The normal Coalition response to revolt had been impossible since the threat came from so many directions at once.

So they'd gained some ground that week, and they'd kept gaining ground ever since.

Slowly and not without a price.

One of the prices was this rural planet had nearly been abandoned. Kyla and Hall had been forced to let their vineyard and winery go—the grapes were growing wild now, and the outbuildings were in disrepair. Cain and Riana hadn't been able to let their ranch go completely a year ago when they'd left to help Desh since the cattle couldn't survive on their own. So Talia and the others took turns staying on the planet to help out. Now that they had control of this part of space, it wasn't a risk to be coming and going.

Rone always stayed on the planet with his and Lenna's children. He still got violently ill from any sort of space travel. Cain and Riana's ranch wouldn't have survived without him.

As if her thoughts had materialized him, she heard a noise behind her and turned around to see Rone walking into the barn. He was frowning. "I was do that," he said in his growly voice.

He spoke their language pretty well for someone who had only started speaking it a few years ago, but he still had trouble with verb tenses, articles, and personal pronouns. Evidently his native language didn't use them.

"I know you were planning to do it," Talia told him, "but I had nothing else to do."

He came to stand beside her, still frowning deeply. He was unlike any man she'd ever known in the way he never tried to hide what he was feeling, not even the polite mask required of normal social interaction. He shook his head at her, clearly disapproving. "Desh yell if Talia hurt."

She laughed and wiped the rest of the sweat from her forehead and the bridge of her nose. "I'm not hurt. And

166

someone needs to help you with all this work. Desh knows I don't want to sit around doing nothing."

"Talia does lot. Stories and plans and ideas." He was smiling now, and respect for her was clear to see on his face.

It made her feel good. Really good. That this strong, good man liked and respected her—not as a sex object but as a person.

Over the past two years, they'd discovered a lot of value in all those stories about uprisings she'd read. She had a whole library of strategies and experiences in her head that they'd used to come up with ideas of their own.

She never would have believed she had something to offer like that.

"Thank you," she said. "But I can also unload some feed occasionally." She breathed in the smell of dirt and animals and old wood. It smelled raw, natural, so unlike what she was used to. "It's not bad work, really."

"Work good," Rone said, nodding in obvious agreement. "This world good."

She felt a little pang in her chest as she thought about the world he'd lost. "I guess this is still kind of strange for you, taking care of animals instead of hunting them, having your wife go off and fight while you stay with the children?"

Rone was giving her a curious look, and for a moment she wasn't sure he'd understood her. Then he said, "Strange, yes. Different but still same."

She cocked her head. "What do you mean?"

He looked around the barn, clearly working through the words before he said them. "World bigger. Tribe bigger. So much bigger. But Rone and Lenna take care of tribe, fight to defend tribe. Still same." He nodded as if pleased with his articulation of this conclusion.

Talia felt a little lump of emotion in her throat as she reached over to put a hand on his arm for a moment. "I completely agree," she said.

Rone looked like he was about to say something, but then his eyes moved over her shoulder, toward the entrance to the barn.

She saw what happened on his face. He simply couldn't hide his feelings the way most men she was used to. In a moment, Rone's face had transformed with a wash of pleasure, excitement, and affection.

He appeared to have completely forgotten Talia existed as he strode past her.

Talia turned to look and discovered the cause of his distraction. Lenna was standing in the entrance to the barn, grinning at her husband.

It had been six months since she'd been back on this planet, six months since she'd seen Rone.

When Rone reached her, he scooped her up into a tight hug that lasted for just a few seconds. Then he released her, turned her around, and pushed her out of the barn with a hand on her back. "Lenna come to bed," he growled. "Now. Rone wait *forever.*"

Lenna laughed and turned her head to wave at Talia as Rone hurried her away. "Good to see you, Talia. Desh is behind me. We'll catch up later!"

Talia stood where she was and laughed out loud, ridiculously happy for Rone and Lenna.

She was very happy for herself too.

She'd only been away from Desh for a month, but she'd missed him. A lot.

She was still chuckling to herself as she stepped out of the barn. She saw Desh's strong, lean figure approaching across the yard.

Even from a distance, she could tell he was tired. Really tired. His shoulders were slumped slightly, and his stride wasn't as energetic as usual.

Every week for the past two years, he'd seemed to get more and more tired.

Still determined but really tired.

She ran over to meet him, and he wrapped his arms around her, holding her for a long time without saying anything.

He felt warm and strong and needy and familiar. She loved him so much.

"How are you?" he asked at last, pulling away enough to look down at her face.

She smiled up at him, her eyes burning with tears. "I'm fine. I'm good. I missed you."

"Me too. I thought this month without you would never end."

She could see that he meant it. He never did as well without her. It wasn't just that she could help him with a lot of things. It was that he needed her support, her companionship, the respite she could offer him.

He'd never been able to find that in any other way. Only in her.

She reached up a hand to cup his cheek. He needed to shave, and there were shadows under his eyes. "You look really tired."

"I am."

He didn't say anything else, but she could see loss in his blue eyes. Something must have happened.

Every person who died weighed on his conscious, as if they were his personal responsibility.

The rebellion was no longer solely in his hands. It had taken a life of its own. Almost half the Coalition Council supported them now, and military experts who had joined them made nearly all the tactical decisions now. It was different than it had been at the beginning, but Desh still felt the pressure of leadership very heavily.

"Are Hall and Kyla here too?"

"Yes. They're with Cain and Riana and the kids. They went to make dinner."

"Are you hungry? Do you want to join them?"

Desh shook his head. "Not right away."

"Okay." She reached down to take his hand and led him toward the main house. "Let's clean up and get some rest then."

This evidently was what Desh wanted to do because he squeezed her hand and walked beside her in silence.

Talia felt a familiar twisting in her chest—worry and knowledge and love and understanding.

He didn't do well without her. He took too much on himself. He got lost in his own intelligence and responsibility and need to make things right.

Only a couple of years ago, those impulses had led him on a suicide mission.

He'd grown and changed, just like she had, but he was still the same man. And it wasn't good for him to spend so long without her.

~

A half hour later, she was sitting on the bed, waiting for him to get out of the shower. She'd taken a quick shower first since she was hot and sweaty from working, while Desh had sat and decompressed. Then he'd gone into the shower and had been there for a really long time.

If he didn't get out in five minutes, she was going to have to go in there and get him.

He was probably just standing there, letting hot water stream over his body. But she didn't know what he was thinking, what he was worrying about, and he needed to get out so he could tell her.

She knew he brooded about his father a lot. He hadn't yet had to confront his father—the man who had betrayed his own son, sentenced him to a planet dump because he'd taken a sixteen-year-old's earnest words about freedom as sedition— but she was afraid one day he would have to confront him. Desh was strong enough to handle it. She knew he was. But he didn't always know it himself.

She was about to stand up and go get him from the shower when she heard the water turn off.

Relaxing, she waited a few minutes until he came into the bedroom with a towel wrapped around his waist.

She smiled at him, and he smiled back.

"Come lie down," she told him, patting the bed.

He didn't argue. He stretched out on the bed on his back, and she lay beside him, turned on her side so she could face him.

"I hope you're not expecting a long, vigorous round of sex right now," he said with an ironic lilt in his voice, "because I'm not sure I'm up for it."

She chuckled. "I'm not feeling very energetic today either." She reached out to stroke his chest. "I'm just happy to be with you."

She felt and heard him let out a long breath. "Me too."

"Did something happen, Desh?"

"Yes. Just a minor setback, but... Can we talk about it later?"

"Of course." She kept stroking his chest and abdomen, putting pieces together in her mind. They'd been in a holding pattern with the Coalition for a few weeks now, and the only real action was on one large planet that had joined them just this month and had almost taken control of all their Coalition bases.

Desh had sent in some of their forces to support that planet. There must have been some casualties.

He would tell her about it as soon as he was feeling better. He always did.

When her gaze returned to his face, she saw he'd closed his eyes. For a moment she'd thought he'd actually fallen asleep, but then the corners of his mouth turned up in a smile.

"What are you smiling about?" she asked him.

"Just happy." He opened his eyes and held hers. "I missed you."

She experienced a warm wash of pleasure. "I missed you too."

"So things have really been okay here for you?"

"Of course. I keep telling you every time we talk I'm doing just fine. I'd rather be with you, of course, but I like Rone and I like helping out here. I really like this planet. It feels... good. The fresh air. The nature. The work." She paused. "I really wouldn't mind living in a place like this, after all this is over."

"Yeah. Me too."

Her fingers were brushing across the tight muscles of his belly. He was starting to get hard. She could see it beneath the towel. "You know they're going to expect you to take on some sort of leadership role, after this is over."

He shook his head, closing his eyes again. "I know. But I don't care. After this is over, I'm going to... do something else. Maybe something with books. I'd love to... study again."

She wanted that for him too. So much she could feel the tug of longing in her chest. "Then that's what we'll do. When this is over, we'll let other people take the reins, and we'll do something else."

He sighed, his whole body relaxed except his cock, which was fully erect. "Yeah. That sounds perfect."

She slowly unwound the towel from his waist. "You know, you never used to talk about when this is over."

He opened his eyes. "What do you mean?"

"Even a year ago, you would talk like this rebellion was all we'd ever do. I think something is different now. You're seeing an end." She stared down at his naked body before wrapping her fingers around his cock. "That makes me happy."

He sucked in a sharp breath at her touch. "I guess... maybe I am. I didn't realize that." His body tensed up palpably as she caressed him. "Oh fuck, sweetheart, I missed you so much."

She was washed with waves of pleasure and entitlement and affection as she saw his body respond to her touch. It still gave her irrational thrills every time she remembered that she was the only one who had ever touched Desh this way. And she was the only one who ever would.

She was hot and excited and pulsing with arousal as she lowered her mouth to his groin.

He moaned when she licked a line up his shaft and then moaned again as she took him fully in her mouth.

"Oh fuck," Desh breathed. "Oh, sweetheart."

She sucked him a few times, thrilled at the way the muscles in his thighs and stomach tightened.

Then he reached for her head and pulled her up so she could see his face. "If you do this for me right now," he said hoarsely, "I'm going to come in about two seconds. And I want to do more than that with you right now."

She nodded mutely, emotion strangling in her throat. She slipped off her robe and straddled his hips.

He gazed up at her, naked adoration in his expression. His gaze never faltered as she lined herself up on his cock and then sheathed him with her pussy.

Both of them moaned—and kept moaning as she started to ride him.

Desh raised his hands to grip her bottom, holding her in place above him, and he rocked up into her with the same kind of focused eagerness he'd had from the beginning. He'd never gotten jaded or controlling in bed. He always poured all of himself into their lovemaking, like it was the most important thing in the world at that moment. Like *she* was the most important thing.

She'd never known sex could be like this—not until she'd met Desh.

She was feeling full and deep and emotional, rather than particularly sexy, so she didn't try to prolong it. She pushed down against the urgent bucking of his hips until she felt a climax tightening. She huffed out her pleasure until the pressure broke, and Desh cried out hoarsely as her pussy clamped down around him.

He jerked and shook through the spasms of his own climax until both of them had worked through the lingering contractions. Then she fell down on top of him, and they held each other, panting and hot and sated and clinging.

It was several minutes before Desh's breathing evened out and he was able to move again. He helped her move off him, and she snuggled up at his side before he pulled the covers up over them.

After a few minutes, she lifted her head to check to see if he was still awake.

He was. His eyes were open, and they met hers with soft fondness.

She smiled. "I did want to ask you about something."

His eyebrows drew together, as if he could hear the slight hesitation in her voice. "What is it?"

"It's time for me to renew my birth control. And I need to... I need to know for how long."

He blinked.

She cleared her throat. "I can do it for five years, two years, one year, whatever. I just need to... need to know." Her stomach twisted as she waited for a response.

They'd talked about having children in theory but never in practical terms, because both of them agreed that they didn't want to have kids while this rebellion was in progress.

The last six months had brought them huge strides closer to their goal. They weren't there yet. Not even very close.

But the end seemed to be a possibility now, when it hadn't felt like that before.

He reached a hand over to cup her cheek gently. "What do you want?"

"I… I want to have a baby with you as soon as I can. Not right now. But as soon… as soon as this is over."

"That's what I want too." He took a breath and then swallowed. "Maybe just do the birth control for a year. I don't think… it's unlikely to be over by then but maybe… maybe we'll be close."

A burst of joy awoke in her heart she'd never experienced before. "If it's not close, I can always do another year then."

"Right. No sense to put it off longer than we need to." His lips turned up in a smile. "And I feel like… being hopeful."

She was grinning like an idiot, but there was no way she could stop. "I feel like being hopeful too."

She did.

She'd lived for most of her life not knowing she was allowed to hope for anything beyond the taste of grapes and the possibility of having her own room.

Her world had grown so much bigger. Harder, more dangerous, but so much better.

And now she could hope—she could dream—of a future that was even better. A future with Desh and the children they would have, in a better world than they lived in now.

Nothing was promised. Anything might happen.

But the fact that anything might happen meant that hope existed.

She wasn't going to live without it again.

ABOUT THE AUTHOR

Claire has been writing romance novels since she was twelve years old. She writes contemporary romance and women's fiction with hot sex and real emotion.

She also writes romance novels under the penname Noelle Adams (noelle-adams.com). If you would like to contact Claire, please check out her website (clairekent.com) or email her at clairekent.writer@yahoo.com.

Books by Claire Kent

Revenge Saga
> Sweet the Sin
> Darker the Release

Escorted Series
> Escorted
> Breaking

Nameless Series
> Nameless
> Christening
> Incarnate

Hold Series
> Hold

Release

Fall

Rise

Standalones

Seven

No Regrets

Finished

Complicated

Taking it Off

Printed in Great Britain
by Amazon